Better Than 8

Fantasy

A Better Than 8 Story

ERIN JAMISON

Copyright © 2011 Erin Jamison

Cover design by: Francesca Zometa

Edited by: Beth Barany, Barany Consulting

Tadpole Productions
Richmond, VA 23222

Printed in the United States of America

ISBN-13: 978-0615504551
ISBN-10: 0615504558
ISBN-13: 9780165460932 (ebook)

First Printing: June 2011

I'd like to dedicate this book to a woman I miss more and more every day,

"Sookie Too Sweet!"

Your memory lives on in the hearts and minds of all of us. They broke the mold when they made you babe!

ACKNOWLEDGMENTS

The author would like to acknowledge trademark recognition
of the following:
ABC Television, Bewitched
Apple Inc, IPod
Warner Bros, The Matrix
Hallmark
Splenda

Phyllis Parker, Anissa M. Ellis, Jason Monroe, Patricia
Guzman, Nina Villalobos, Antonia Manibusan, Ana Punla,
Vanessa Christian, Randall Coleman, Beth Barany, Alene &
Barry Kercheval, Judah & Davina Larrimer, Karen Gilbert,
and Dana K. Sullivan. Thank you all for being really great
friends and family!
I want to give a big shout out to all my fellow bloggers,
authors, networkers, reviewers, and the Indie community.
Without the support of community, where would we be?
To my muse, and you know who you are, thank you for
being so inspiring.

CHAPTER 1

"How long has it been, Amara?" my girlfriend Stacey asked. Then she continued without waiting for a reply. "Let's see ... the last man I heard about wanted to be your maintenance man while keeping his main squeeze. What was his name?"

"Adrian, I think ... " Nicole chimed in waggling her eyebrows. "And you know everybody needs a maintenance man ... to you know ... maintain certain areas."

Chuckling along with the rest of my friends, I looked around my living room at them. All four of them were in relationships, save me. It had been four years since I'd been with Adrian, since he'd gotten married.

I looked around my living room at my four girl friends. We had all been friends it seemed like forever but in reality, it had only been six years. They were all the sisters I never knew I wanted and never had until now.

We had all worked together in one capacity or another. There were many friends I would say were associates or friend, the term used loosely. These girls, though, I loved.

There was Nicole aka Nikki, the party planner. The very one that had planned this little girls night we sometimes had on Sunday nights at my cozy two-story Tudor house not far from downtown Mountain View, an hour south of San Francisco. Nikki was the youngest of my friends. She was half white, half Mexican, 26 years old, tan, shorter than five feet tall, and a brunette, usually.

Then there was Vanessa aka Nessa. Nessa was brown skinned, 28, big brown eyes, with a mischievous sense of humor. She was also the whitest black girl I had ever known.

Then Stacey, the red headed, stubborn, "I ain't taking no shit off nobody" kinda girl. She was 40 and a long way away from mellowing out.

Last but not least was Charlene aka Charlie. Charlie was the quick-witted, 30-year-old, strawberry blond shit talker.

I felt my face heat up at the mention of Adrian as I gathered the dishes off the table and took them into the kitchen. I grabbed the strawberry cheesecake. On my way back I passed by the floor-to-ceiling hallway mirror and paused. My cheeks were flaming from all the talk about Adrian. My skin was naturally all peaches. I had long dark brown wavy hair, hazel eyes, petite nose, and a full lush mouth. I was cute and curvy. I could admit that to myself.

After four years of being single, I had trouble explaining to myself why me, 35-year-old Amara Simmons, why I was still alone. Except that Adrian had burned me bad.

"Mmmmm," Nessa hummed as she bit into the strawberry cheesecake I had served. "I swear I don't understand why you're still single." I shrugged.

She continued. "I mean you're gorgeous, small waist, full breasted, phat ass; for a white girl. And ... you can cook. Hell, I'd marry you simply so I can have cheesecake!"

Amid a chorus of laughter and the clink of wine glasses lifted in agreement with Nessa's statement echoing my own thoughts, I offered a suggestion. "I simply haven't met the right one." I sat with my head resting on the back of an overstuffed brown suede chair with my legs stretched out in front of me on a matching ottoman.

"The one. You make it sound like that movie, The Matrix. Is that it?" Charlie asked sardonically. She had a mischievous glint in her eye as she sat on my sofa, one leg crossed under her, the other swinging back and forth. "Are you waiting on your version of Neo, or are you stuck in the Matrix?"

"Very funny Charlie. I'll know him when I find him that I'm sure of." I sat up quickly, planted my feet on the floor, and leaned forward. "You know I've been wondering though, what if I find Mr. Wonderful and he's not as well, hmph umph, equipped as I would like."

"Mara, OMG! I mean, are you looking for a porn star? Hell, you'll never find anyone if that's the criteria you're measuring against," Stacey said and flipped her red hair over her shoulder.

"That's pretty vain, don't you think?" Nikki asked. She shifted her petite self in the middle of the white sectional swirling her wine glass. "That's like a guy saying a girl has to have a set of DDs or something for him to be satisfied. Isn't it possible to fall for a guy or girl that doesn't meet all your preconceived notions?"

Stacey leaned forward in the recliner and looked at the rest of us, sitting on the couch facing her, her green eyes flashing. "Well, hang on now. I think you like who you like and for me at least, I speak from experience. 'To thine own self be true!' "

We laughed at her attempt to mimic Shakespeare. I nibbled on my cheesecake. It was divine. If only I could find a man as easily as I could bake.

Stacey stood up and went behind the corner bar for another bottle of chilled wine. "I do think that it's about knowing yourself. Me for instance, I know I like an average-sized man. I can get off no problem." She stopped mid pour and glanced at me. "Mara here on the other hand needs a man the size of a bus to get her off!"

"No, no. I'm not looking for King Kong!" I exclaimed. That gave me a moment's pause. That actually didn't seem like a bad idea. My friends watched me. I hummed loudly, for effect and raised an eyebrow. We all burst into a fit of giggles.

"You know, hell … " Charlie said. "I heard about this website. It's a dating website like a lot of them that are out there already."

A chorus of groans and a lot of "Oh no! Here we go! Not this again!"

"No, seriously. I have a friend that told me about it and she's talked to a few guys from the site. She's going out on a date with one of the guys this weekend." Charlie added.

"Charlie, I'm sure it's a great site but what makes this site different from the next dating website?" I asked as I scooted back into the cozy chair and tucked my legs under me.

"This one, you get to pick how big a lover you're looking for!" She nodded knowingly. The room was quiet as we all exchanged looks with one another.

"You mean—" I started.

"Yep. That's exactly what I mean. If you need a seven-inch lover, that's what you put. The site is called www.betterthan8.com. You may have to live outside your comfort zone and upgrade to a size eight to use the site though," Charlie said with a sly grin. "What do you think?"

"Well, I don't know what to think." I said. But I was curious. *Should I?*, I wondered.

"Well, I know what I think!" Stacey sipped her wine. "I know that if I wasn't happily involved and completely sexually satisfied with my Adonis of a boyfriend, I would register in a heartbeat."

"I concur!" Nikki said and raised her wine glass. We all toasted. I hid my smile in my drink.

The next hour passed with lots of tasteless dick jokes and lots of giggles and laughter. Finally, sometime after midnight, it was time to kick them out and I hugged and kissed my girlfriends goodnight at the front door. Back in the kitchen, I loaded the dishwasher and wiped down the kitchen counters, smiling to myself. *Better than eight, yeah right!*

I liked a tidy house, but decided to leave the vacuuming for the morning. For now, I needed a nice hot bath and warm bed, in that order.

Upstairs I started the bath water and drank the last glass from the last bottle of open red wine we'd had for dinner.

Wrapped in my thick bathrobe, I tested the water to find that it was entirely too hot. I decided to wait a little to let it cool.

Even if it was just for me, I went about lighting my vanilla-scented candles in glass jars placed strategically around the bath and counters. The bathroom looked like a scene from a movie, I thought with a smile, *"Ambiance."* By the time I came back, the water would be just right, and the smell would be pungent with vanilla.

While I waited I sat down in front of the computer set up in my bedroom. I checked email, paid a couple of bills online and was just about to sign off when I thought of the website again. *"What the hell!"*

I bit my nail with apprehension, took a deep breath, closed my eyes and pulled up the site. After a minute, I peeked open one eye and then both. The site looked normal, just like a normal dating website. Nothing triple X about it. I clicked the "About Us" link and read. How they wanted to give everyone a chance to meet someone they would really be interested in and to help get that "part" of the conversation out of the way. The site explained that it was often difficult for men to discuss their size with women seriously as most tended not to believe them. And for the woman, what was she supposed to do? Ask for his name and then ask for his penis size? With betterthan8.com, that conversation could be gracefully taken care of and the women could at least anticipate that the man they met from the site could be well endowed.

"Makes sense," I said out loud. *You're talking to your computer. First stop, the funny farm.*

"Here goes nothing!" I said aloud and clicked on the Join button. I had to list characteristics about myself. I needed a title and a description. What kind of title would get me noticed? I bit my nail again as I thought about my comment from earlier and decided it was perfect. I typed in: Seeking King Kong.

That ought to get somebody's attention. I needed a description as well. I typed: I'm cool and fun. I like a variety of music. I like to dance, go to the movies, and read. I love to laugh. I need a well-endowed man to tame my inner freak! *The truth is the light ... and I so need to be set free.*

I raised an eyebrow with a grin. *So true.*

After completing my description I was taken to a search menu. I searched for someone 28 to 45 years old, some college, fit, not married, and hit enter. Quite a few profiles came up but it was the third one I got to that made me stare. My heart started pounding.

His complexion was golden brown. He wore corn rows, had brown eyes, a slim nose and a gorgeous mouth. He was in profile but you could still see most of his face.

Those lips. I licked mine involuntarily. He was wearing a shirt with no sleeves. It was obviously a picture that had been taken in the summer time. He was standing in the sun, squinting a little against the light. He was obviously fit, with strong muscled arms but not a body builder's physique; instead his long limbs were rather sleek like a basketball player's lean body.

I looked again, more like stared, took a deep breathe, ignoring the butterflies in my stomach, and clicked on his profile.

His profile was titled "Looking for a Connection." I skimmed. Unmarried, check. Looking back at his face, Gorgeous, check. College educated, check.

His description made me smile.

> I like to stay physically fit so I work out a lot. I work as a financial consultant. I work hard and play harder. Despite that, I like quiet time. I'm an avid reader and sports fanatic. Let's take a little time to get to know one another.

I sighed. He sounded perfect. Taking a chance, I clicked the link to list his as a hot pic. What would he be like?, I wondered, you know, in bed? I shook my head. I'd probably never meet him. His details were probably fake anyway.

I logged off the site, turned off the computer and went into the bathroom. It was time to settle into my just-right bath.

I let my bathrobe drop on the floor. It had been a long time since I'd let a man touch me. That guy, that hot guy from the website, I would love for him to touch me. I slid into the hot water, just at the perfect amount and temperature to engulf my entire body into the generous porcelain tub. I leaned back and lifted one leg to soap it. The water slid down my calf. There really was something so luxurious about a bath. I thought back to his profile.

He'd written he was ten and a half inches big. That was huge but my oh my ... if only I could.

I let my imagination have its way with me as I lay back in the tub and closed my eyes. I trailed my hands between the mounds of my bosom, my stomach, my hips, my heat. He had muscular powerful arms and, from what I could tell, broad shoulders and a strong back. And probably a tight ass. Just that image of him made me think of him leaning over me, his strong arms holding up his sculpted body, his lips on mine as he pounded my body.

I could feel the moisture starting to pool in delicate places. I squeezed one breast as I trailed my hands between my thighs with the other. *Would his voice be accent heavy?* His golden brown complexion hinted at a Latino heritage. I slipped my finger past my folds and delved inside. *Would he speak with no accent at all?* I pinched my nipple and moved my finger in a steady circular motion. *Did he speak Spanish in the throes of passion? Mi amor.*

"Hmmm," I groaned out loud. *Would he utter a sound as I tightened around his cock?*

I could almost hear him grunt as he pounded me harder. I bent my head forward as I groaned and bit my lip. I pinched my nipple harder and my hand moved faster.

I whimpered and panted, "So close." So caught up in the movie playing behind my closed eyelids, I could hear him say with a husky command, "Baby now ... come for me now."

My body clenched and spasmed as I cried out. I sighed and stretched languidly into the now cooling bath water. My heartbeat was slowing from the fast staccato it had been. His gorgeous body stayed with me little longer as I experienced the after-orgasm shakes.

I sat up in the tub and smiled, happy and satiated, for now. I quickly finished my bath, dried off and climbed into my bed. Tomorrow was another day and I was tired.

I would probably never hear from the guy even though he was hot as sin. I scolded myself. I didn't need trouble like that in my busy life. I half hoped I wouldn't hear from him but half hoped I would.

Signing up for the website had been an impulsive thing to do. In the morning, I'd delete my profile. I fell asleep dreaming of a man that could make my body ache in ways I was so eager to experience. But probably never would.

CHAPTER 2

"I've got the best news. Wait till I tell you!!" Katherine, my business partner, said as she followed me into my real estate office the next morning. She handed me my steaming mug of coffee. "You won't believe it!" She closed the door behind us.

"I'm sure I will believe it where you're concerned, Katie." I sipped the warm brew and smiled into the cup. "If you tell me what it is, can we get some work done afterwards?" She was my right hand, my back up, and my all-around go-to gal. "I really need—" I forgot what I was going to say when she stuck her left hand in my face.

I was speechless at the size of the rock that was on her left ring finger. I was no jeweler but that was a least a couple of carats. I looked at her, mouth agape.

Katie exclaimed, "I know!" in her thick Indiana country twang, so exaggerated I sometimes had to hang onto her every word to understand her.

Then I managed to close my mouth and smile appreciatively. Katie was cute. She was taller than me, about 5'7. Small breasts, small waist, long legs, and the biggest bubble booty I'd ever seen on anyone. She was a down home Southern chick.

"Well?" I finally found my voice. "What did you say?"

When I'd told her I was moving to California, she said, "When do we leave?" She'd struggled alongside me over the last few years as we had built my real estate business. Last year, we were finally in the black. I had worked and saved every cent and finally taken out a loan to do what I had always dreamed: become a real estate entrepreneur. And Katie had benefited as much as I had. She had a home of her own, respect among her peers, and she had finally found a man she loved.

"Well, I said yes of course silly! I'm getting married! Can you believe it? I can't believe it. I never thought he would do it. I mean I've been threatening to leave if he didn't do it 'cause I ain't gettin' no younger. I took and told him." *Him* sounded like heemmm. "That I was only giving him one mo year and after that, I was out. And I meant it!" she said sucking her teeth and grinning.

I smiled at her. We were both Southern but she sounded a lot more Southern than me. Despite her colorful vernacular she really did love Douglas.

"Shoooottt! Think I'm gone wait around on him all day long, he got another thing coming."

Not wanting to begrudge her happiness, I put aside my files and ignored the mountain of work on my desk in my office. "Okay, come on. Give me the scoop!"

Katie squealed with delight and plopped down on the plush burgundy chair by the window to tell me all about her weekend. "Well, I came home Friday and I was tired. We had a really long day Friday, remember?" Nodding, I motioned for her to continue. "I had no idea he had a weekend getaway planned. We went up to the Sonoma wine country to a bed and breakfast there. It was perfect, romantic. We shopped, went to art galleries, took long walks. I still had no idea what he was up to." I gave her the most sardonic twist of my lips I could muster and she said, "Ok, well yeah, I was hoping."

"So then what?" I prompted, playing my part as the nosy girlfriend.

"The place we stayed at had the most beautiful gardens but you know I'm a freak about bees so we took a walk through the gardens at night. It was backlit with ground lights and there was a fountain with statues. I swear it was straight out of a movie. We walked the entire garden and I started up the stairs and he pulled my hand to turn me back around. He dropped to one knee and asked me to never leave him and to be his wife," she said with tears in her eyes.

"Wow! That boy must have gotten pointers from someone because I never would have figured him to be the romantic type."

"I know. Who knew? But ... he done good," Katie said with a sniffle.

"Okay. So now that we've had our Hallmark moment here, can we get some work done?" I said with a smile.

"Nah unh. Not until you tell me about your weekend," Katie sat back and crossed her legs. She was just as stubborn as I was. I knew we weren't doing anything until I spilled the beans.

I sighed and dove in. "It wasn't anything spectacular." Breaking eye contact, I shrugged and squared some contracts on my desk. "I worked on some contracts, set some appointments to show some houses for this Saturday and the girls came over for dinner last night. They were the highlight of my weekend actually. We had a good time." I purposely left out the late night trip down fantasy-o-rama lane I'd gone down last night.

"Did they rag you about being single?" Katie asked, smiling the smug smile of the soon-to-married.

"Don't they always!" I chuckled.

She watched me missing nothing. "Well?"

"Well what?"

"What gives Mara?"

I sighed. "Charlie suggested a dating website."

"Oh no, not another one. Dis one's gonna be the one, right? You gonna find your prince charming on this site because it's different from all the others right? Tell me you laughed at her."

"I did." I nodded vigorously. "But ... I ... ah ... checked out the site anyway."

"And?" Katie asked pointedly, tapping her foot against the short table with neat stacks of interior design and gardening magazines.

"It **is** different. It's called betterthan8.com. You can pick how big ... you know," I said, waving my hand and looking away. I could feel the heat on my face. I was going turn into a chili pepper before I got this out.

"You're kidding?"

I shook my head and looked up at Katie. She was smiling as I said, "I, ah, I, um, registered for the site last night." And I hadn't deleted my account this morning. I just couldn't. My curiosity just wouldn't let me.

"You did? Wow!" Katie uncrossed her legs and sat up. She looked me straight in the eye and said, "I always knew you was a freak. It's always the quiet ones you gotta watch out fo." She laughed her full belly country laugh.

I laughed right along with her, a little nervously though, and said, "You don't think it's weird? I mean it really looks like a dating website and not some creepy, sleazy kind of site where you just hook up for sex."

"No, I don't think it's weird. It's kinda nice actually. I don't think I ever told you but I met dis guy once, really liked him ... thought I was falling in love wit 'em. We did a lot of heavy petting and I was under the impression that he had quite da package. But he was all balls, little pecker."

"Oh, no!" I didn't know who I felt sorrier for. Not him for his size but for his ego. My friend was not known for her tact but then again, how were you supposed to react to that? "What did you do? Better yet, what did you say?"

Katie shrugged. "You know I started to just rag on him but I cared about him at that point. I decided that I could at least give him a good send off so, I had sex with him." She smiled broadly. "It was enjoyable but I was never really satisfied. I mean he was great with his hands and mouth and all but I didn't have an orgasm. It was just nice. Just nice."

"So what happened after?" I leaned forward.

"We went our separate ways. He called a lot and I became really busy. He stopped calling after while." She squared a stack on contracts on my desk.

We sat there in silence for a few moments, she lost in her memories, and me reeling with the memories of Adrian and the way we had ended. I didn't want to experience that kind of disappointment again.

What Katie said next surprised me. "That's exactly why this site is great for you."

"Why?"

She leaned toward me eagerly. "You get to pick what you want. You at least have a better chance of getting a well-endowed man with this site. Besides, how big are you trying to go?"

I felt a hot blush creep up my face. I said nothing.

She smiled knowingly. "Just be careful." She wagged her finger in the air. "There are some men out there that have big 'uns but they ain't got a clue on how to use it. All they know how to do is poke somebody with it."

I felt my face get hotter, if that were even possible. "The biggest guy I've ever had was nine inches and he was a big dude but it was good. Really good!" I said huskily.

"Alrighty then!" Katie slapped her thighs and grinned. "On that note, I think I'll get back to work. I hope you meet someone you really like and who will be good to you, Mara. You deserve it." She stood and smoothed down her bright orange skirt. "I've got the contracts on my desk and I'll get through them today and let you know if they're missing anything." Katie gave me a wave goodbye and left my office, shutting the door softly behind her.

I thought about Adrian, who would love to fill the position of a maintenance man. I fanned my face with a contract. Just thinking about Adrian made me hot and wet. He was married now and he hadn't chosen me. But God—

the man had a body that was made for fucking. I squirmed in my chair trying to relieve some of the heat. I picked up a contract to review and sighed.

My itch would have to wait. It was time to get back to work.

CHAPTER 3

It had been a long day. Mondays were often the busiest day in real estate. After two house showings, one deal in the process of bidding, and three contract close outs later, I was finally home. Other than regaling me with the tale of her engagement at the beginning of the morning, Katie and I both had worked through the day without a break. It was good to be home.

I laid my purse and briefcase bulging with paperwork in the brown suede chair near the staircase. My home was decorated in earth tones with touches of elegance placed strategically around. I loved my crystal-based lamps with petite brown satin lamp covers with gold brocade fringe. With a smile I glanced up at the double-mated print in a custom gold frame that I had recently bought. My salary couldn't keep up with my taste for the finer things but I managed to sneak in an item or two.

I kicked off my shoes and went to raid the fridge. Although I pretended to be Betty Crocker on the weekends, during the week, it was usually sandwiches, salads, or leftovers. I quickly made a club sandwich, carried it upstairs and changed my clothes to my standard at-home attire: tank top and shorts. I studied myself in the mirror, admiring the diamond necklace around my neck. It was a single solitaire necklace, just a little something to wink at you. Adrian had given it to me. I brushed the diamond and shivered. It fell right into my décolletage, which I was pretty sure he'd been fully aware of when gave it to me. He'd been such a passionate lover. I thought for sure he was the man for me. Our times together had always led to bed. For a moment, I could practically smell his musky male scent.

Ugh! I had put him firmly out of my mind during the day. I couldn't afford for him to distract me from my business or my life anymore. I had to move on. Four years, for God's sake!

But at home, it was different. Unless I immersed myself in work all the time, it was way too easy to get lost in my memories of what it had been like between us. We had met through a mutual friend and had become good friends. That had led to something more on my part, and a good time on his. That I didn't want to admit. I had been the lady in this life, right up until he picked someone else to be his wife. I knew then that he had never been serious about me like I had been for him.

The phone ringing broke me out of my reverie.

I dove across the bed, bouncing a little before reaching for the cordless phone. I answered the phone breathlessly, "Hello!"

"Hello beautiful!" The tenor of that voice I knew so well.

"Adrian!" I exclaimed. I couldn't help it. Knowing how this conversation was gonna go, I moistened right away in anticipation. Didn't they say that women were at their sexual peak mid thirties? It was certainly true for me.

"You sound out of breath love! Did I interrupt anything?" he asked in that deep voice of his.

"No, of course not. I just got home and changed. I dove across the bed for the phone so I'm a bit breathless but I'll be okay. So how are you, handsome?" I pulled the phone away from my face to hide my panting and smiled. Here we go again, and I wouldn't be denied a little phone time with the hottest man I knew, who was calling for me, only me. I just needed to hear his voice.

"I'm good. Even better now that I think about your sexy ass laid out over the bed. Long legs, thick thighs, and that ass!! Mercy me. Mmph, mmph, mmph!" Adrian exclaimed.

I should have realized I had left him an opening and he wouldn't hesitate to take advantage of it. I'd asked for it.

Eye roll. "Oh here we go!" I said sarcastically with a grin.

"Don't blame me. You're the one that brought it up," Adrian said. "You knew I wouldn't be able to resist. I could talk about that delectable body of yours all night. Better yet I'd like to be fucking you all night. Now that would be a lot better." His deep voice rumbled.

Inward groan. But I couldn't deny the reality. "And how is your wife Adrian?" Emphasis on the wife part.

He continued as though I never spoke. "Remember the time when I came to see you and you were at home not expecting anybody. You saw that it was me and you didn't want to be rude?"

"Yes, but—" I tried half heartedly to interrupt.

"You came to the door in a wife beater and shorts. Really short shorts. Blue I think. The wife beater was white but old so it was see-though. I don't think you realized just how see-though it was. It was tight too and showed everything. It was a beautiful sight—one forever imprinted on my brain." Adrian smacked his lips right into the phone.

I wasn't dressed too much differently than I'd been that night. At least my tank top was solid. You couldn't see through this one. I said nothing, just grinned and laid back. He certainly knew how to make my body respond without even touching me. My nipples were perky but then again what was new? Anytime I ever thought about sex, my nipples would perk up as though they were looking for attention. Some things go hand in hand though 'cause whenever that happened, the water works work start down south. I bit my lip to stop myself from moaning. I knew if I suggested or even hinted, he'd have phone sex with me in a minute.

Adrian continued, teasing me. "You tried to cover up and I asked you to not to hide from me, to show me. You remember? That was the night. The night I kissed both your lips. That night, I finally got to taste you. I still remember the taste—sweet like peaches," Adrian practically growled.

Son of a bitch. He knew. He knew he was turning me on. He knew I was getting wetter by the second. Turn about was fair play however. Using the sexiest voice I could muster, I said, "I remember. I remember that night I dropped to my knees and felt you through your jeans. You were so hard. I never knew, had no idea, how big you were really were. I unzipped and pulled down your pants and took you in my mouth. Remember? Remember how I wrapped both hands around you and stroked you. Sucked you in and out of my mouth? The way you looked, head back, eyes closed, mouth open, your hands tangled in my hair. It was a sexy sight," I said with a husky voice.

Taking in a shaky breath, he said with a devilish smile in his voice, "Oh, you play dirty."

Smiling, I rubbed my legs together. "Is there any other way to play? Besides you started it."

"Oh love, I enjoy playing the games that we play. It is such a pity you keep me away from you. We are both civilized adults. We can restrain ourselves. I'll be a perfect gentleman. Invite me over."

"Adrian, no," I said softly. I shook my head, even though he couldn't see me.

"Mara please, I miss you," he whispered.

"Adrian, no. We've talked about this and that's over now." Taking a deep breath, my voice became stronger. "You're married. You chose someone else, remember?" I tried as hard as I could not to sound bitter but it still came out with more emphasis that I had intended. "You get married because that's the one you want and it's supposed to be enough. We both know you haven't been a saint during your marriage. I'm beginning to think that I wouldn't have been enough for you. Naomi's a good woman, Adrian, and she loves you. None of us are perfect, including you." I huffed out a breath of exasperation.

"I know. I know I'm not perfect. God knows I'm not perfect but Naomi isn't you Amara. I chose the wrong woman because you scared me. I have no idea why you're still single. You're the perfect woman, love. You cook, you're tidy, you're successful, you work hard, you're sexy, phenomenal in bed might I add, beautiful, smart, and you smell amazing."

That made me laugh. "You remember my smell?"

"Yes! Abso-fucking-lutely!" he exclaimed. Ok, that made me giggle. "Seriously Mara. Sometimes, I smell you on the wind and I think that you've come to visit me finally but you're not there. I wake from a dream and reach for you except you're not the woman I hold in my arms. I love Naomi but it's not the same. I love, want, and crave you."

"I don't know why you're telling me this now. You've been married for four years. You know why I had to put distance between us. The way we were together was intense. How could I not fall for you?" I said with a catch in my throat. "You chose another woman, Adrian! Damn it! And I didn't find out you were dating, much less engaged until six months before the wedding. You proposed while you were still banging me! Yet I'm the one you crave? Yeah because you can no longer have me." I gripped the phone tightly, my voice rising at this old argument. Fuck, I was angry now and I didn't want to give him that kind of power.

He was silent for so long that I about ready to hang up. Then he spoke, softly. "I was a fool and I didn't realize what I had. Even then, I didn't want to let you go. I thought you knew that I didn't think we were exclusive, that I was seeing someone else. Everyone knew.

"No! I didn't know. Dammit!"

But Adrian continued as if I hadn't spoken.

"I kept telling myself to break it off with you but every time I saw you I wanted to touch you and that hasn't changed."

"I know. I know. After all this time, I'm just as aware of you in a room as you are of me. I know you want to touch me and I want you, too." I hated that fact. But it was true. "And which is precisely the reason why I don't come around and I don't want you to come see me. You know that! I can be your friend, Adrian. We can be friends because that's what we were for so long. If you really need me, I'm here. As a friend, but only as a friend," I said firmly, tired. The same old conversation we'd had many times before.

"I'll take what I can get Mara. I want to be in your life and if this is how I can be close to you, I'll take it. I wanted to hear your voice. I didn't mean for this to turn into a heart to heart," he said with a little nervous laugh.

"It's okay. I guess some things needed to be said on both our parts. I still love ya," I said lightly. I'd given up on having the kind of relationship with him I wanted years ago and only felt a little sad that he wasn't the *one*.

"And I you love, I do. Take care and know that the phone works both ways, Mara," Adrian said.

"Duly noted Adrian. I'll talk to you later. Goodnight."

"Goodnight love," he said gently and hung up.

I hung up the phone and my hand lingered on the device as if I could touch him. I knew that God said we would be tested, but when would the test be over because this was becoming torture?!

I looked over at my sandwich. I had only taken one bite out of it but had little appetite now. I picked it up anyway and made my way over to my computer. Might as well check my email while I was here. I had to get Adrian out my head.

There was an email from Nikki to the other three girls suggesting we do the evening gathering again the following weekend at my house. I shook my head at my friend with a smile. I could wait to tease her in person about offering my house up like she lived here knowing full well that she would know it was fine. Mi casa, su casa.

Picking at pieces of turkey from the sides of the sandwich, I noticed an email sent from member services.

The subject was "You have mail in your inbox." Confused, I clicked on it. The email read:

> You have been contacted from a member of betterthan8.com. Click this link to return to the site.

I sat there for a minute confused. Somebody had read that ridiculous crap I had put on there—and actually responded. I was almost a little afraid to read the email. But my curiosity wouldn't let me turn away. I went back to my inbox. Another email said that someone had chosen my picture as a hot pic. *Oh well! Here goes nothing.*

I clicked the link. Signing in to betterthan8, I expected that I would only have one email but there were five.

"Oh wow!" I said. I shifted in my seat, nervous and a little excited.

Sandwich forgotten, I bit the edge of a nail absentmindedly and clicked on the first email. It was a guy from London—as in the UK. His email read:

I got a monster-sized cock waiting for you baby.

"OK, ewwww! Delete!" I pressed the delete button quickly. The second one was from a guy in the United States at least—just on the other side of the country, New York. His email said:

I always wanted to do it with a white girl. Eight inches of huge loving here babe.

"Oh yeah, just what I always wanted! Oh and by the way guy, 'do it'—so mature," I said with disgust. The third guy was nineteen. I didn't even read his. I didn't do jail bait. The fourth one was at least in the same state. His email read:

I waNa c u nekid. Im so hott for u.

"Delete!" No third grade edumacation graduates for me, no siree.

"Why did I let Charlie talk me into this? One more to go. Maybe this one writes with crayons!" I said sarcastically to the computer.

I opened the last email expecting more of the same. I read it and was confused for a moment. Moving my hand away from the delete button, I read it again for comprehension. It said:

Can you play Ann to my King Kong? My name is Sevastien and I'd like to get to know you better.

He made a play on my words. Cool. He was intelligent. I clicked on the link to see his profile picture and it was the hot guy, the same one I had listed as a hot pic.

The same guy I'd fantasized about in the bath. Hot didn't begin to describe him. I gulped trying to concentrate. Holy ... !

"Well would you look at that?" I said aloud, a little breathless. I clicked the link that would show me who had me listed as a hot pic. Same guy.

"This could be the start of something very interesting." I smiled. My heart continued its little pitter-patter. This could be fun.

I hit the reply button and typed:

> So you got the joke and I see you have a sense
> of humor as well. You're a very attractive man.
> I'd like to get to know you as well, Sebastien.
> My name is Amara and I look forward to
> hearing from you.

Sevastian had to be a typo. He probably meant to type Sebastien. And I gave him my direct email address.

As I hit send I squirmed in my seat and thought of taking another bath. Sebastien was as delicious as my fantasy man. Better, hopefully, because he was real.

I hoped he'd respond. My fantasy man had a face, and a name and a hot ass body. Fantasy man and I had a date in the boudoir. I got up from the computer and went to run the bath water.

CHAPTER 4

"Chop chop! Morning review. My office, five minutes," I announced passing Katie's office. It was Tuesday morning and I liked to hit the ground running. "And bring your assistant!" Katie and I had a morning review every Monday morning but we'd gotten off track the day before. In our review, we talked about deals that were closing, any specifics that were holding up closing, and cases that she needed me to facilitate, which was almost never, and any potential issues.

Five minutes later, Katie walked in and greeted me, "Warden!"

"Smartass." I nodded my greeting with a grin.

Introducing her new assistant Katie waved to him and me. "Amara, Michael. Michael, Amara."

Michael appeared to be more of a mouse than a lion, perfect for Katie. She'd be nicer to him if she figured she could bully him but if he gave her the slightest challenge, she'd have his nuts for lunch.

He was dressed in khaki pants and yellow dress shirt, had a pale complexion, glasses, blue eyes, and sandy colored curly hair, recently trimmed. But no tie and an open collar. That was a problem. My office was professional attire required which meant men had to have ties. I was dressed in a long navy skirt down to the ankle with a split to the knee. I had on a crème silk spaghetti strap tank top with a navy and white crème crepe blouse over it, the first couple of buttons undone. Katie was wearing a green cotton gathered dress cinched on side of her waist showing off her curves quite nicely. I didn't like to chastise my employees; it was far easier for them to just follow protocol. But I gave Katie the eye just the same.

Holding up a hand, Katie said, "I already told him. He's aware and will come dressed appropriately tomorrow, won't you Michael?"

"Yes ma'am. My apologies," he nodded, looking contrite.

"No problem. You'll be okay for today." I assured him." So what's cracking Katie?" I asked moving on to business matters.

"First things first! Coffee?" She handed me my Caramel Macchiato.

"Oh bless you!" I relaxed after the first sip.

I opened my mouth again, but she jumped before I could speak. "And yes, I added extra Splenda." Nudging Michael she whispered, "She's a sugar junkie."

"It's so true. I've been trying to kick the habit for years," I said clasping the cup lovingly.

Katie mouthed, "Not really."

"Okay she's right, not really. So can we move on from my sugar habit missy?"

"Don't get your knickers all in a bunch. Drink your coffee," she said motioning for me to drink up. "Peeples, Mendez, and the Mason deals will all close by the end of the week, no problem. The Marrow deal is pending proof of income and before you ask, no I don't need help with it. She's coming in this afternoon."

I nodded still worshipping the coffee cup in my hands.

"There is a potential problem with the DeVante deal," she cautioned.

"What's up?" She had my full attention.

"Michael?" Katie said. Looking from her to the new guy, I raised my eyebrows and gave him a concerned look. That deal would give me some clout. It would establish me and my company as a major player in the area, not just some small here-today-gone-tomorrow type of real estate company.

"What's up Michael?" I said firmly. Jesus, if he pushed his glasses up any further they were going be imbedded in his head.

"Eric DeVante has tied up a considerable investment in a potential resort area in Puerto Rico. The local natives are raising a stink because they are accusing him of being just like the rest of the greedy Americans. They think that he just wants to break ground there to line his pockets while having no concern for the economy of the island, the people, or the environment. It's been going on for the last six months and I doubt the issues will be resolved in the next couple of weeks, which will affect or rather effectively delay—prevent—close," Michael said. We were working on closing two of his properties in Northern California.

I nodded at him and turned to Katie. "That's a multi million-dollar real estate deal and we stand to make a substantial commission from the sale, not to mention the credibility it will garner us. What can we do?"

"You mean, what can you do, right? We both know you could sell lava to a man in hell. I suggest you talk to him. You might be able to help him negotiate or at least come to a resolution," Katie said.

"Katie, maybe you missed the mountain of paperwork behind me, much less marketing the business, meeting clients ... You know I'm buried." I waved my hand over my shoulder.

"Yep, I do know. But you are the one, dearest, that chooses to operate with such a slim crew. You take work home all the time. When are you gonna admit that you need an assistant?" Katie asked. Katie handled the processing with the banks, title clearance and all the important behind the scenes paperwork of the office.

I mumbled into my coffee, "When hell freezes over."

"Yep, that's what I thought. Look, you wanted to know what we needed to get the deal through and we told you. What you do with it is up to you," Katie said dismissively.

I sat up. "I'll make a phone call and see if we can help him out in any way," I said, mentally putting on my big-girl shoes. "If that's all, let's get back to work. Thank you for the play by play. Good work." I added my regular pep talk for Michael's benefit that Katie had heard plenty of times. "That's all a part of due diligence and it's our responsibility just as much as it is for the customer to inform us. I appreciate your efforts. Katie, thanks for the coffee!"

Michael smiled and walked out first. Almost out the door Katie looked back and said softly, "Hey?"

Thinking she wanted to talk about Michael I said, "What's up?"

"Any potential candidates from the website?" Confused, I looked at her with furrowed brows and scratched my head.

She said, "You know, THE website."

I caught her drift and said, "Oh, yeah, that website. Maybe. I'll let you know."

She pointed at me. "Be sure that you do!" and left my office. I shook my head at the now vacated doorway.

Several times throughout the day I thought about checking my email but instead I really tried to focus on work. At the end of the day right before I left work, I remembered that I had promised to make a phone call. Plugging in DeVante's cell phone number I got from his case file, I dialed him on my way out of the door.

I had just finished placing my overstuffed briefcase into the back of my Honda Accord, when a man answered, "Yeah?"

Confused I said, "Hello? Mr. DeVante?" Silence. I plowed ahead. "This is Amara Simmons from Excellent Realty." Silence. "We're handling the sale of your property in Atherton and the acquisition of the estate in Sebastopol in Sonoma County. We met—"

"Yes, Ms. Simmons, what is it I can do for you?" he said tersely, interrupting me. Eric DeVante's voice sounded a little gravely, like he was or had been a heavy smoker. I'd forgotten that about him.

"I just wanted to touch base with you. We are nearing the approach of the closing process with both properties and we just want to ensure –," I began.

"I'm sure everything is in order Ms. Simmons," he interrupted curtly.

I climbed into the car, closed the door and took a breath before continuing. "Mr. DeVante, we pride ourselves on being thorough and that includes doing our own due diligence. Any pending investments that you may have a large investment of capital in may affect and or prevent closing. Do you anticipate any foreseeable roadblocks sir?"

Chuckling, he answered, "May I call you Amara?"

Surprised by his shift in attitude, I answered coolly, "If I may call you Eric in return, certainly."

After a moment he said, "By all means. Amara, I am quite pleased with you. You came highly recommended to me."

"Oh?" I raised my eyebrow at that.

"I was told you were quite intelligent, witty and tactful. They failed to mention however that you have beauty as well as brains," he said with a smile in his voice.

I said nothing. *Yeah sure, whatever. He was probably just saying that.*

He continued. "I was expecting this phone call actually. In a business dealing such as this, if I became aware of a potential issue, I would have made the same phone call. I fear there may be some cause for concern. It has been a long process and the way negotiations are going, may be further still."

"Well, I'd like to offer our help in any way we can to avoid any potential impact to both projects," I offered. It was the polite thing to do and no doubt he would leave it at that. He had to have lawyers and negotiators at his fingertips.

The man was a millionaire, many times over. He certainly didn't need my expertise on the matter.

"I appreciate the offer and I'll remember that." Was it just me or did that sound a little ominous? "I'll be in touch."

The next thing I heard was a dial tone. I sat there for a minute thinking about how the conversation had gone. He was a bit of a puzzle. He came off as abrasive and then suddenly became charming. I wondered about which one of those was an act. People don't just switch on and off like that but then again, I didn't know many millionaires. I had a niggling suspicion that I would be hearing from Dr. Jekyll/ Mr. Hyde sooner rather than later.

I sighed as I started the car and pulled away from the curb. It was times like these I so wished I could be just like the character Samantha, from Bewitched, that I could just wiggle my nose like she did on the show and everything would be right with the world. I enjoyed the television show immensely as a child. Despite the fact that I was a grown woman, I still tried to wiggle my nose like her. I glanced at myself in the mirror and tried to do it several times, just like always. And just like always, I looked like I had an itch that I couldn't scratch.

Fifteen minutes later when I pulled into my driveway, I was still smiling at the looks people had given me as I drove down West El Camino Real turning my face this way and that to get my nose to wiggle. Yep, and I was an entrepreneur. *The job title didn't say you had to be mature*, I thought to myself and opened my front door.

"Ahhh, home!" I said aloud to the empty cozy living room. Not quite ready to eat yet, I went upstairs, showered, and changed into yoga pants and a tank top. Wanting to be more comfortable, I grabbed my laptop off my desk and sat in the middle of the bed Indian style and logged in. I skimmed the list of emails and saw right away that he had responded. I bit my lip with a grin and opened the email, my heart pounding.

I logged into the site and clicked my inbox. His reply read:

> Amara is it? What a pretty name for such a
> pretty woman. A woman who likes variety,
> sex, big men, and is cool too? Sounds a little
> too good to be true.

I replied and typed:

> I could say the same about you. Young, fit,
> attractive, single, educated, and financially
> stable. Those are not qualities found in a lot
> of young men today.

I hit the send button and waited for a reply. Instead a chat screen popped up on the bottom right of the screen and a dialogue box appeared asking permission to chat from none other that Mr. Sexy himself. I raised my eyebrow and glanced at the monitor that had a webcam built in. I covered it quickly and ran across the room. I yanked a comb through my hair and hustled to put on some mascara and lip-gloss and went back to the computer and accepted the request to chat via instant messenger. Right away Sebastian typed.

> Mr. Sexy: Hi Sexy.

> Me: Hi yourself. I didn't expect you to be
> online right now.

> Mr. Sexy: I know. I was pleasantly surprised
> as well. How are you?

I grinned as I typed my reply. I glanced back at the cam but there was no image. Maybe he didn't have a cam. I had gotten all dolled up for nothing. Oh, well.

> Mr. Sexy: I'm doing well. Work has been
> challenging but I'm sure it will all work out
> eventually. Oh, btw, my name is Sevastien.
> Seva for short.

I gasped and rushed to make amends.

> Me: I am so sorry. Sevastien is so
> uncommon. My apologies.

> Sevastien: No big deal. LOL. As you said, it
> is uncommon and a common mistake many
> people make but its fine. It's Puerto Rican
> and I'm what you would call, "Black Latin."
> So Amara? Does it mean something?

> Me: Well, I'm sure but no one ever
> bothered to tell me and I've never been that
> interested in looking it up myself. It's just a
> name. No big deal.

I shrugged. I was half laughing at myself. I went to forums but usually just looked at conversations. If and when I started to get noticed in a forum and started receiving private messages to chat, I'd usually just leave the room. Here I was up typing a conversation and reacting to it as though he was right in front of me. Well, I realized he kinda was right in front of me. Hmmm. This was kinda fun.

> Me: So Sevastien, you like to read I saw on
> your profile. Seems like more and more
> people I ask say they don't read. Are you
> the quiet introverted type?

> Sevastien: LOL. Ha Ha! Introverted. Who
> me? Yeah right? I can't even fix my face to
> tell that lie. No doll. I am not introverted.
> Maybe a mix. I do like things my way
> however.

> Me: So, you're spoiled?

> Sevastien: No, but I would love the
> opportunity to spoil you though. And ... I'd
> love to see more pictures of you.

> Me: Yeah, I just bet you would Mister. So, you been on the site long? Ever hooked up with anyone from the site? I just registered a few days ago.

> Sevastien: No, I haven't been on the site long. An ex-girlfriend recommended it to me. She told me it was for large men and well ... I'm a large man so I decided to try it. I haven't had a profile on here much longer than you have.

> Me: So how long has it been since you were in a relationship? It's been four years for me.

I swallowed and sat back. It'd been a long four years without. I leaned forward to read Sevastien's response.

> Sevastien: Three for me. I dated a woman but it was a long distance relationship and they never work. I had a project going on in Atlanta and I flew back and forth from there to San Diego.

> Me: Wow. Must have been some woman to make you fly 3000+ miles just to see her.

Did I sound jealous? Hopefully I didn't even, though I already was. Damn! I wished some hot guy would fly 3,000 miles just to see me. "Lucky bitch," I said.

> Sevastien: I didn't just fly there to see her. I went more so for work. After the project was done we tried to continue it but the distance, never seeing each other, and the cost of flying back and forth to see one another just proved to be too much. What about you? What happened with your last relationship?

I looked at the screen for a long minute. I started to type and deleted. Started again and stared.

> Me: I wasn't the woman for him. We're still friends and he's married now.

I didn't want to say: "Well see, I was in love and thought we were gonna get married and he dumped me and married someone else, literally right under my nose."

It was a sore topic for me to talk about at length because that meant I had to acknowledge that I'd had blinders on and I should have been smarter. I was trying not to still beat myself up about the Adrian situation but I didn't want to forget lest I make the same mistake again.

> Sevastien: Why weren't you the woman for him? I think any man would be lucky to have you. You sound great. Oh and btw, pictures pls.

I absentmindedly started looking on my computer for a picture to send him. I had a few photos of the girls and me at the beach. They'd convinced me to wear a bikini. I looked good but it sure didn't cover a lot. What it did show was my curves. There was another picture where the girls and I had gone out for the night to a club and they talked me into taking a sexy picture. That night Charlie had dressed me in a slinky silver gray dress with a high neck, sleeves down to the wrists, and an open back down to the top of my bottom. The dress was only mid thigh. We had all done a number of sexy poses but this one they had told me to give them my best come hither look across my shoulder with my hair hanging long in soft curls and waves down to mid back. Shimmery silver pumps accentuated my well-toned legs. I sent both to him in an email and went back to the chat window.

> Me: I sent you a couple of pictures. As for my last relationship, I have high hopes for him. I'm not sure the woman he chose is

enough for him. He always seems to be looking around instead of in front of him. Hopefully, he'll realize what he's got. He married a good woman.

Sevastien: Wow. You're still friends with the dude? I don't know many women that could be that adult about the whole thing. You knew him a long time?

Me: Yeah ... and he knows me better than anyone; better than my girlfriends. But he's just a friend. Now.

Sevastien: So four years is a long time to go without getting your needs met. You and ex-dude gotta secret lover, FWB, kinda thing going on?

I smiled. Friends with benefits. Yeah right.

Me: No ... ain't no Me and Mrs. Jones thing going on over here. I told you. We're friends. Just friends.

Sevastien: So ... you use toys?

I cleared my throat and tapped my fingers on the keyboard. I could be adult about this.

Me: Yeah, I do.

Sevastien: How large is your biggest one?

Me: 9. The biggest one is 9.

I should have probably changed the subject. I didn't know him and he didn't know me. If I really wanted a relationship that meant anything, I shouldn't be looking for it on a website like this but ... I couldn't help but linger and see where it would go, curiosity ever my guide.

Sevastien: You ever had anyone as big as me, baby?

Cocky much? Maybe I could steer this back to a playful area.

> Me: How do I really know you're as big as
> you say you are?

> Sevastien: I'll be happy to show you. King
> Kong ain't got nothing on me.

I was already shaking my head at the computer and typing into the chat window, "No, that's ok. You don't have to show me." I had typed it and was about to hit send when my inbox lit up. I sat there for a second and then opened the email. Inside were three pictures. One was of his abdomen. The man had washboard abs. Hot! Instead of a six-pack he had an eight-pack. OMG! I touched the screen wishing I could be touching him instead.

"Whoo," I said out loud. Was it me or was it hot in here all of a sudden?

I opened the second picture and stared at it. I kept looking, trying to make sense of the image. I knew it was the lower half of his abdomen 'cause I could see his abs at the top of the screen but it looked like one image. I kept looking and thought to myself that it must literally look like a third leg. Just about then the image started making sense and I could see that his member went past mid thigh in a deflated state. It was only when I went to swallow that I realized my mouth was hanging open.

"Holy shit," I whispered. My panties went from moist to soaked in nothing flat. I moaned in anticipation.

The third picture was him smiling a sly knowing smile showing brilliant bright white teeth, staring out from the camera as if he were looking right at me. His caramel skin was unmarred of defects. It was a stunning photo.

I glanced back at the chat window and smiled. He'd open my pictures.

Sevastien: Daaaaammmnnnn baby. I'd like to dedicate myself to worshipping your ass. Jesus! Where do you put all that?

Me: LOL. Yeah, the Lord blessed me I must say.

Sevastien: Amen is all I can say.

Me: Yeah well, he seemed to have blessed you as well. Speaking of where do you keep all that? And what do you do, tape it to your leg?

Sevastien: No, LOL.

Me: How do you hide that? I mean what do you do, buy pants 3 sizes too big so they can be baggy in front and not show off your package?

Sevastien: No, I wear short briefs and there is no hiding it really. When I'm dressed in clothes it's not that bad but forget swimming. There's just no hiding that but I don't try either. I'm proud of my manhood.

Me: Uh huh. I bet you are. I betcha you've scared women away with all that haven't you?

Sevastien: You know I tell women I'm a big dude but they don't believe me. I try to prepare them as much as possible. But yeah, I have had some women completely freak out. I know I'm big and I go real slow. The Lord blessed me with length and girth so I know I gotta be careful. What do you think? Too big for you? I'll understand.

Me: Well, I-I-I mean, I-I-I'm saying, well maybe...

I used my hand to gesture to the screen then typed.

Me: Well I don't know.

Sevastien: I've had some women who have really enjoyed their time with me. They say they've never felt so full.

Me: Yep ... uh huh, no shit.

Fucking hell that dude was equipped to be able to bring any woman to orgasm and if he wasn't careful to make her bleed too. I was never so glad as I was in that moment that I had met him and saw him over the Internet because I would have hated for him to witness me freaking out. I could just imagine the women he'd scared away after he had gotten them all hot and bothered, dripping with desire taking one look at him and putting their clothes back on and backing out of the room. I'd even bet money some women had literally run away from him. Dude was huge. And then there was me. Me, who hadn't had a man in four years, was soaked down to my pants from wanting that man.

Sevastien: Amara, do me this one thing.

Tonight, I want you to take out your toys.
Do you have one or two?

Me: Two.

Sevastien: Where are you in your house?

Me: In my bedroom. On my bed.

Sevastien: Are you wearing clothes?

Me: Yes.

Sevastien: Take them off. Take them all off. I want you naked. Put the computer on the bed beside you.

Me: Seva ...

I hesitated. Should I play along? One thing I knew for sure was that I didn't want to end the conversation. I looked back at the screen.

> Sevastien: Trust me. This will be good.

I was a grown woman, older than him and here I was gonna take off my clothes and masturbate just the way he wanted me to. Well, put like that, it sounded hot. I smiled and took off my tank top, pants, and panties. I typed, "BRB." Be right back. I rushed into the bathroom for a towel and ran back to my room, my boobs bouncing, my nipples tight. The tops of my thighs between my legs were already wet. I reached into the back of the nightstand and grabbed both dildos.

I spread the towel and settled down on it and typed:

> Me: OK. I'm back.

> Sevastien: Are you ready baby?

> Me: So ready!

> Sevastien: That's my girl. We'll start off slow. Just imagine for me. Rub your hands down your body. Light. Slowly. Barely touching.

I took in shallow breaths. My skin tingled, hypersensitive. I'd never done anything this erotic. I ran my hands down the inside of my thigh and grazed my lips.

> Sevastien: No touching down there yet babe. We'll get to that in due time. God, you've got a beautiful body. Do you shave down there babe?

> Me: Yes.

> Sevastien: Hmmm. Yeah, I thought you did. I want you to look at my picture too. Can

you imagine what I look like when I'm aroused? Hot for you ...

I moaned.

Me: Yes.

My fingers shook a little as I typed.

Sevastien: Are you wet baby?

Me: Yes.

My inbox lit up again.

Sevastien: I sent you something baby.
You've got me excited.

I opened the file. It was a video of him stroking himself by hand. He was making long strokes and there was a pearl of liquid glinting right at the tip. I wanted to lick that. I hadn't realized when I had done it but I had one hand on my breast and the other on my clit.

Sevastien: See how hot you make me baby?

I typed back awkwardly with one hand.

Me: You make me hot too. I want to lick you. I want to taste you.

Sevastien: Oh, I so want you to but we have plenty of time for that. This night is about you. I want you to take the first toy and suck just the tip; pretend it's me. Just wrap your pretty lips around the lip. Play with it babe. Can you do that for me? Suck me slow.

I did. Oh my God! This was hot.

Me: Yes baby, yes!

Sevastien: I haven't forgotten about the other one. Do you want to come baby? Will you come for me?

Me: Yes. Please.

I was panting, my heart racing with anticipation.

Sevastien: Take the other one and slid it into your hot, dripping, wet box baby. Pretend that it's me. Take it slow. Feel every inch. I'm filling you up ... so full. Easing you into it. Rocking you slow baby.

I was moving the dildo back and forth and I wanted faster. I dropped the dildo from my mouth and typed.

Me: I don't wanna go slow. I want it faster. Harder.

Sevastien: I aim to please. Does your toy vibrate? If so, turn it on.

I obeyed and turn on the vibrator. "Oohh." I spread my legs and worked it back and forth and looked back at the camera eyes above the laptop's screen.

Sevastien: Faster baby. Move it faster. Your legs are wrapped around me and I'm pounding your body. Pounding that pretty pussy. Your wrapped around me like a fist ... Take one hand and work the dildo and use the other to get yourself off. Come for me baby.

"Soo close," I said shakily. My entire body was tight with the need to come.

Sevastien: Come. Come. Come for me baby. Please.

"Oh ... oh ... ooohhh, ssss!"

Sevastien: Now baby. Come for me now!

My body bowed back involuntarily and I cried out as my body clenched and climaxed. I was still clenching and unclenching around the dildo as I reached down to turn the vibrator off. I glanced back at the screen just as he was typing.

Sevastien: Did you come?

Me: Yes.

Sevastien: You are one sexy woman.

Me: I can't believe I just did that. God, I never should have done that.

Sevastien: Don't start judging what we just did. It was beautiful. I loved it. I only wish that I had been there to see it. I wish I could have heard you. I bet you sound sexy.

Maybe he couldn't see me, his side of the webcam was dark. Didn't care. It had still been hot.

Me: You're welcome to call me. I like you. I don't want you to think I go around doing this with every guy I talk to online. I don't typically talk to people online so this is a first for me.

I typed in my phone number.

Sevastien: Baby, I like the way we're getting to know one another. This is more intimate. You usually say more this way than you do when you're thinking about what not to say. This can often be more truthful. I will call sometime just ... not yet.

Me: I thought you said you were single.

I was starting to feel foolish. I never should have done it. And I notice he didn't give me his phone number.

Sevastien: I am single. I promise you. I hope you understand.

Me: This is definitely unconventional but I'll give it a shot.

I was unsure but what the hell? I shrugged. I glanced at the clock on the screen.

Me: Oh shit. Did you realize it's after midnight? We've been talking for a good 3-4 hours.

Sevastien: You know what they say. Time flies when you're having fun and we were having lots of fun.

Me: Very funny. Don't quit your day job. I have to say goodnight. I have to be up early in the morning.

Sevastien: OK. Sweet dreams Mara. I'll be thinking of pounding that sweet body of yours well into the night.

Me: Good night Seva. Thank you for a wonderful night. Until next time ...

Sevastien: Next time being tomorrow morning, tomorrow afternoon, tomorrow evening. Oh, this isn't over. Not until I get a taste of that sweet ass for myself.

Me: You talk a lot of shit for someone 400 miles away. Nothing between you and I except time and opportunity.

Sevastien: As soon as I'm able, we'll rectify that.

Me: All right big daddy. Goodnight.

Sevastien: Good night and sweet dreams baby.

Me: You do the same.

I logged off and put my computer back on my desk. I took a shower, cleaned my toys and put them away, then got into bed. I lay there replaying the whole conversation and make out session. It had been so hot. I brought a pillow next to my body and hugged it. No substitute for the real thing but maybe … just maybe I could be a little excited.

Who was I kidding? I was a lot excited just thinking about next time.

Throughout the next three months, Sevastien and I emailed one another, chatted through IM, and played almost every day. He had such a great personality. It literally came to life off the screen, like words do in a good book. He was so attentive too in our play sessions. It was like he knew how to make me hot and just when to push me over the edge. It was incredibly erotic. Time flew by.

There I was apprehensive about even keeping my profile on the site until I realized that three months had gone by. I had to admit that the online chats, the emails … it made it more personal, more intimate. It really made me feel close to him. I was always eagerly awaiting the next email, and the next.

CHAPTER 5

I struggled through my front door with three bags of groceries hanging off my arms and hands and rushed to answer my ringing cell phone. "Hello," I said slightly irritated, trying to settle my bags on the kitchen counter.

"What are you wearing?" the caller said with a husky voice.

"Hi Adrian," I said with a smile.

"Hey! How did you know it was me?"

"You're the only perv that ever calls me, Adrian," I replied chuckling.

"Funny ha ha. Everybody's a comedian. Don't quit your day job," he said sarcastically, echoing something I'd typed to Sevastien. Then he switched gears and his voice dropped into a husky whisper. "How are things, love?"

"Great! I mean really great!" I replied happily. "I met someone."

"Really?"

"Yeah! He's 30. He's Latin, single, no kids, funny, considerate, gorgeous, hot, sexy ... you get the idea."

"Yeah, I get it, you like him," he replied sarcastically.

"Yeah, I do," I sighed wistfully.

"Somehow, I never pictured you and a Latin man, much less a younger man. But then again, that's probably because I was picturing you with me," Adrian said in his deep purr.

"Yeah well. Dreams over, buddy, time to wake up," I replied sarcastically. "I meant to say Black Latin. He corrects me all the time."

"So, how did you meet?" It seemed he really wanted to know and wasn't being sarcastic.

"We, ah ... met on a dating website," I hedged. I didn't want to tell him which website. "Charlie recommended it and we just started emailing one another. He's pretty close to wonderful actually," I said matter-of-factly.

"You sound like a woman in love," he said softly.

Giggling, I said, "Don't be silly. I've never even met him. I haven't even talked to him yet over the phone although I've given him my number. I don't even know what his voice sounds like. Hell," I said with a snort. "He could call in at work and I would never know it was him."

"Uh huh! Just be careful."

"Adrian, don't be jealous. You had to know this would happen someday. I need you to be a friend about this. Be supportive." I waited to hear how Adrian would react to my plea. I'd worried about it. What would he do? How would he act when I finally moved on? Would this be the end of our friendship? I held my breath.

Finally Adrian spoke softly. "I'm always here for you love. I want you to be happy, though it kills me to say it. Even if you're not with me."

I snorted disbelief and started shoving groceries away into my cupboards one-handed. "What amazes me is that you still talk about us as though it was a possibility." *How many times were we going to have to have this conversation?*

Adrian said nothing but I swear I could almost hear what he wanted to say. *Couldn't I wait?*

"I'm not getting any younger and a woman could die of old age waiting on a man to come to his senses," I half joked.

"No matter the age, Mara, you are and will always be a beautiful woman." His voice deepened as he said that and I knew he was thinking about us in bed, how it had been, how he'd made me quake from orgasm. I felt my body respond to his sexy purr. I paused in putting the milk in the fridge as a jolt of desire sparked through me. I pushed it away.

"Adrian, stop."

"What? It's true! The man that finds himself lucky enough to have you will be a lucky man indeed," he said with mixture of melancholy and passion. "I just know you, Mara. You fall quickly, you always have. You like who you like and when you don't, there is no discussion. It's just over. You already like this dude way too much. How long have you guys been emailing each other?"

I swallowed, but didn't answer right away. There was silence on the line while he waited for me to speak. I finally answered slowly. "A while. Three months."

"Wow! Three months ... and you haven't mentioned him to me until now. I just talked with you two weeks ago. You were afraid of what I was gonna say?"

"Yeah, I was. I'm not in love with him but I'm in like with him a lot. I'll at least admit that."

"It's more than like Mara, but I think you have to come to that discovery on your own. I want you to think about what I've said. I think you're more into him that you've admitted to yourself. I'm here for you either way," he said a little sadly.

"I know and thank you," I said. We said our good-byes and hung up the phone.

Adrian was just being negative. Really, it was to be expected. As long as I remained single, as long as I allowed him to go down memory lane with me without being assertive enough, things would always be the same between Adrian and I. I had to admit to myself that the dynamic of our relationship was within my power to control. I valued my friendships. Among male friends, Adrian really was it. He knew everything about me. He knew what food I liked, how I took my coffee, my fashion sense, how I thought, how I would react. And he knew my desires, things I wouldn't even tell my girlfriends. A friendship like that was too invaluable to let go.

I stacked my Glory Collard Greens and Corn Niblets can goods on the shelf with the label facing outward in perfect order, row by row, can by can, I thought about my relationship with Seva, the nickname I had started calling him instead of typing out Sevastien.

"Relationship?" I said aloud. "Yeah right." It was a relationship of sorts. It was good, delicious even. Every day all day, I looked forward to his emails and banter back and forth.

During the day at work, I had gotten in the habit of leaving my email open and periodically checking it in between phone calls and meetings. Often we talked about our day, like funny things the girls had emailed or called me with. I shared everything important with him ... Katie's wedding plans, my own goals and ambitions, funny stories from my past. Though I had never used his name in any email exchange, Seva even knew about Adrian.

I stopped short with a can of corn held in midair just shy of the shelf, struck by something that hadn't occurred to me until just now. *Had I been the one perpetuating the conversation?* Before I even finished the thought, I knew the answer was *yes*. If he didn't email me in the morning, I would email him. Most often it was me starting the conversation. He was always responsive but that could just be him being polite.

"I've structured my whole weekend to be at home," I said aloud to the cans in the kitchen. But I was always at home on the weekend. Right. That was a bluff even I wouldn't buy. How many times had I checked my email today?

At least three or four times. I actively chose not to count the two or three times I had checked from my smart phone.

Oh my God, I seemed so desperate. I picked up the phone to call Katie for an opinion and stopped mid dial. Holding my thumb down on the receiver, I already knew the answer and I already knew what she was going say. She would tell me the same thing any of my girlfriends would tell me, the same thing I would tell myself.

"Don't put all your eggs in one basket. You need to get out more," I mimicked aloud. "Yeah, I do," I muttered as I clunked my home phone back in its holder on the kitchen wall.

Hang on, had I just answered myself? Oh, I definitely needed to go somewhere! *That's it! I'm outta here before I start questioning my sanity.*

I would start putting the onus on him. I had been out of the dating game too long and had forgotten proper protocol, the one basic thing in male and female interaction. I needed to allow myself to be chased. Stupid, but necessary.

Gotta make him work for it! Grabbing my keys I left the house, jumped in the car and headed for the mall. Some people eat when they're upset, others go to the gym. I shopped. It really was the only time I ever went to the mall. Otherwise, I made most of my purchases online. Plus driving gave me time to think rationally. I was angry with myself. Here I was nearly half in love with a man that was probably not as into me as I was for him. Thinking back to the website and how we met three months ago, if you could even call it meeting, I had to be fair. Both of us still had active profiles. Other women on the site had eyes. They would see the same thing I saw. I knew I wasn't the only woman who had contacted him. I had tried to be nonchalant about it and had even suggested he should put a full facial picture, one with him looking directly at the camera, on the website and that would probably get him more responses. The man was sexy and his smile ... he could talk my drawers off any time of day I was pretty sure of it, and had many times in the last three months. My own inbox had filled up with quite a few men but none that I was interested in. Adrian was right. I liked who I liked.

He's not my man. Hell, I don't even know his last name, I admitted to myself. But, I knew a lot of things about him, at least what he told me. He had brothers and sisters, wanted a family, he was single, and was packing in the department that counted. Mentally chastising myself for having my mind in the gutter, I reminded myself that there was more to the man that just his package. Raising my eyebrow at myself in the rear view mirror as I drove, I spoke out loud, "Oh but what a package!"

I put aside my desire for love and a real relationship and focused on what I could control: shopping.

CHAPTER 6

It had been two months, two whole months and I hadn't heard from Sevastien ever since I stopped initiating all of our contact. I was miserable. *Nothing!* I fumed as I climbed the stairs unbuttoning my blouse, tired from a full day's work. Damn Adrian for making me question myself. I had been content with my rose-colored glasses and the perfect bubble I'd been floating on for months before he popped it. For the last two months, I'd refrained from initiating any conversation via IM or email. Seva probably had probably thought I was desperate.

And to boot, the DeVante deal was showing further signs of conflict. I had checked in with DeVante a couple times over the last two months and it seemed his hands were just as tied as mine were since the pending deals couldn't close until his Puerto Rico deal closed. At this point my business was not going along smoothly, like I'd hoped. And neither was my nonexistent love life. I stood in front of the mirror slipping off my blouse and skirt to reveal my black bra, panties, and thigh highs with my heels still on. I looked at my reflection as my dark brown hair settled in soft curls over my shoulder and caught a gaze staring at me from my bed.

I swiped the silver plated hairbrush from the dresser and held it up, ready to strike. Fear propelled me as I whirled around, "What the f—!" Quickly I realized who it was. "Adrian!" My heart pounded with anger and fear.

"Be still my beating heart. I don't know what is more alluring: the sight of you or the thought of touching you. I haven't even touched you but I remember how soft you are. God, you're sexy." Adrian smiled wide at me from my bed. He was stretched out on my covers in the center of my bed.

I looked away. "I am so not in the mood," I said hotly, staring at the wall. My cheeks felt like they were on fire. "You scared the shit out of me! Dammit!"

He slipped off my made bed and approached me. "No need to be frightened babe, it's only me."

I snatched my robe off the hook, kept my eyes averted and stepped away from him. I felt my nipples harden. My mouth watered. I swallowed hard, frustrated at my body's response. "Adrian, you're naked. We are sooo not doing this!"

"You always seem to be struck speechless when I'm naked so I wanted to see if it would free you of your inhibitions."

"Adrian, your being married is not an inhibition. It's a fucking roadblock!" I snapped.

"One time Mara, one last time!" he pleaded.

"You've gone too far, Adrian. I'll make coffee and meet you downstairs." I stepped toward the stairs then stopped and spoke over my shoulder, hugging the robe around me. "It's your choice. You can get dressed and leave but that's it. We're not friends. Or, you can get dressed. We'll have coffee and I'll forget you ever disrespected me like this. Your choice."

I waited. He said nothing.

"You've got 5 minutes," I said and flew down the stairs.

Fuming, I stopped to get dressed in the laundry room off the kitchen. I kicked off my heels, yanked on jeans, slipped on a tank top and a loose button down shirt. At least I was completely covered. "Of all the cotton picking nerve ... " I muttered. I took a few calming breaths, arms crossed, and leaned against the washing machine.

When I entered the kitchen five minutes later, he was sitting at the island in the center of the kitchen nursing a cup of coffee, dressed in his standard t-shirt and jeans. He stood and opened his mouth to speak. But I held up my hand to him. I so didn't want to hear it. He sat.

I clenched my jaw. The sight of him seated in my kitchen was so familiar. It was in this very kitchen where I had gone down on him. I kept waiting for the pain but ... there wasn't any. I was still pissed but I had expected to hurt. There was an old wives tale that said to get over someone you loved you had to fall for another. *Maybe ... no. Couldn't be,* I thought. I wouldn't let myself even finish that thought. Better not to analyze that just yet.

I moved on to safer topics: food.

"I happen to have your favorite dessert: a sweet potato turnover." I had stopped to throw a couple into the oven when I came downstairs to find clothes and escape Adrian. "Can you grab the vanilla ice cream from the freezer? I'll serve 'em up," I said with my back turned to him. We worked in silence. He already knew his way around my kitchen. I laid out the plates. He scooped the ice cream. I plated the dishes with turnovers and placed a plate in front of him. I turned off the stove, took a deep breath, turned around and raised my eyes to look him in the face for the first time since I spotted him in my bedroom.

I had the feeling he'd been staring at me until I met his eyes.

"I'm sorry Mara for more than just my behavior tonight. For all of it." Adrian took a deep breath.

I considered him for a moment and nodded my head. "I know. Let's eat."

He sat back in the chair, relaxing a little. Using his spoon, he cut off a piece and put it in his mouth with an audible groan. I couldn't help but grin at that.

"I take it I've still got it?" A grunt was all I got in response. We continued eating in silence with an occasional grunt until he finished it all and picked up the plate to start licking it. Throwing a table napkin at him, I admonished "Manners! Would you like another?"

"I'll take one to go."

I got up and reached under the cabinets for containers and asked nonchalantly, "Where's Naomi?"

He was silent for a moment. Then he finally answered. "She's out of town visiting with her girlfriend in Florida." He turned away to take his dish to the sink.

"While the cat's away, huh?"

"Something like that. More so I just missed you."

Moving around to the sink where he had finished drying his hands, I hesitated. He reached out and intertwined our hands. Gently urging me forward he whispered, "Have I lost you love?"

I watched his face, looking for some trace of cockiness or some indication that he wasn't being sincere. But he was being completely serious and totally open. I wanted to say, "Never," but instead I went to him and wrapped my arms around him silently. I laid my head on his chest and he hugged me tightly and squeezed. I could feel the tension he was holding.

I finally answered into his firm and strong chest, my voice hoarse with emotion, "Nah. I think I'll keep you around for a while yet."

He laughed and I felt his deep sexy rumble that I'd always loved to hear from him.

Stepping out of the circle of his arms, I turned away to the counter to pack up two more turnovers for him. Over my shoulder, I said, "Oh and by the way, give up the key."

He snapped his fingers and grinned. "I almost made it."

"Not even." I held my palm for the key. Once he placed it my hand, I gave him his turnovers and escorted him to the front door. I hugged him.

He took a deep breath. "You still smell amazing, Amara."

Ignoring him, I said, "Why don't we make a standing coffee date at the coffee place a block from your office? We'll meet for lunch. You down?"

"I am so down. It's a date!" Adrian smiled broadly. I held up a finger with a silent warning and he held up both hands. "A strictly platonic coffee date with a really dear friend," he added.

"Exactly! I'll see you on Friday," I said.

"Friday it is!" Swooping down quickly he kissed me full on the lips.

"Hey!" I yelled.

Laughing as he walked out the door, he yelled over his shoulder, "See you soon love."

"Jackass!" I yelled back.

I smiled as I shut the door and headed up the stairs to bed.

All in all, that ended a lot better than I thought it would have. At least I got along with one male in my life.

But what about the other man in my life? What about Sevastien? Maybe I wasn't enough for him. Maybe he wasn't really looking to settle down. Maybe I was too neurotic. It didn't matter. I still wanted him. Daydreamed about him. Fantasized about him nearly every night where it was just the two of us and he made love to me all night long. Other times there would be two of him. On those nights, I usually woke drenched in sweat. I wanted more than anything for him to call but at this point I just wanted to an email, an IM even, from him.

God! It would be nice to be in a relationship. It didn't have to be marriage but a committed relationship with a man that loved me. Was that really too much to ask for? I wondered if he missed me too, as much as I missed him. Would I ever find a man that belonged to me?

CHAPTER 7

"He did what?" It was Sunday, over a week since Adrian had snuck into my house unannounced, and the girls were over including Katie. I was telling them how Adrian had surprised me.

"I woulda took and told him—" Katie began.

"We all know you woulda took and told him a thing or two with your old country ass!" Nessa said mockingly.

"Keep on hear. You 'bout to start some shit and I'm gone finish it!" Katie said threateningly. Nessa blew a kiss at her.

"You guys are supposed to be playing nice, remember?" I shook my fingers at them.

Katie and Nessa were as different as night and day, one just as a feisty as a hornet and the other should have been a comedian. They couldn't be trusted to be around each other five minutes before the fireworks started.

"I done already said my piece. As I was saying before I was so rudely interrupted—" Katie said rolling her eyes at Nessa. "I would have told him to get the fuck out."

"I did." I jumped in to cool the heat between two of my best friends. I told them what happened, how I gave him a choice, and how he chose to remain friends.

"I don't believe it!" Stacey said staring at me.

"Me neither!" Nikki said.

"What?" I looked around the room at each of them.

"The man breaks into your house, gets into your bed naked, scares the shit out of you, walks around the joint naked, tries to seduce you and let's not forget he's still married and you serve him pie?" Stacey said with confusion and anger.

"You sure it wasn't another kinda pie you served up Mara?" Nikki asked.

"Well, there was no need to be inhospitable," I joked. "Besides, he still had a key. Which I took back."

"So Mara, did you ever try the site out?" Charlie asked, switching topics. "I've been so curious to ask but figured you would have brought it up by now."

"Yeah, actually I have," I said as I glanced over at Katie.

"No shit, really?" Nessa sipped the night's special, a white wine. "And you never told us?"

"Yeah, it was no big deal," I answered.

"Uh oh, what happened?" Stacey said.

"Nothing happened." I shrugged, toed the rug and looked up at my friends trying to keep all emotion out of my face.

Nessa looked over at Katie. Katie held up a finger, "Don't start," she warned.

"You're awfully quiet all of a sudden," Nessa said to Katie.

"What? Is there a crime in being quiet? The woman wasn't even talking to me and here you go," Katie said.

I reached over and patted her knee. "It's okay. I'll tell 'em."

"Tell us what?" Charlie and Nikki said in unison.

"I met a guy, great guy. Gorgeous, funny, sexy, cocky, very very well endowed, supportive, etc." I waved my hand in a dismissive gesture. "It's probably easier to be a great guy though, through email rather than in person."

"Wait. I'm confused. It's only been a few months, right?" Charlie asked.

"More than a few. We emailed each other for three months straight, every day, morning, afternoon and night.

Often we were saying good night to one another through email. I haven't heard from him in the last two months. I miss him." I picked lint off my pants and swallowed down the lump in my throat.

"Sounds intense!" Nessa said.

"I think it sounds romantic," Stacey said. We all turned toward her. "What? I like romance," Stacey said crossing her arms with a huff.

"Right." Charlie said with exaggeration, stringing out the word to last longer that it should.

"I think it sounds weird," Katie said. I started picking imaginary lint off my chair, too.

"Why is it weird?" Nessa asked.

Katie looked at me and everyone else in the room did the same. Clearing my throat, I said quickly, "He never called." I watched their faces.

Nessa and Katie both looked pissed off. Charlie and Stacey both looked taken aback.

Nikki didn't look fazed. "I'm sure it's fine. Is he still emailing you?" she asked.

Again, all eyes on me. I said quickly, "No."

Silence.

"I don't understand," Nikki said.

"Welcome to the club dear 'cause neither do I." I sipped my wine and gulped past the lump in my throat that wouldn't go away.

"So you guys exchanged pictures right?" Stacey asked.

"Yep."

"And you sent each other naked pictures right?" Charlie asked.

Cheeks flaming I said, "I was never completely naked but mostly, yeah."

"And he sent you pictures of his penis?" Nessa asked.

"God Nessa, have some fucking tact!" Stacey exclaimed.

"Well, I mean, come on. What are we talking about here? How big was dude anyway?" Nessa asked.

"Come on guys. She doesn't ask you how big the men you've dated or are dating are," Charlie defended.

"No, it's okay. He's—ah ... ten and a half inches." I felt my checks flame again and tried not to squirm in my seat. "He's rather proud of it. He wouldn't mind you knowing."

He'd get a kick out of me and my friends sitting around talking about how well endowed he was. He'd think it was funny.

Sputtering and coughing, Stacey finally found her breath. "Excuse me?"

I nodded and repeated, "Yep, ten and a half inches."

Nikki said, "Holy shit."

"Well, I say good riddance. We would have been visiting you in the hospital after they sewed your ass back together," Katie said.

"Fucking hell!" Nessa held her arm up. She was staring at it, trying to gauge how big that was. "Dude, that's as big as my arm. That's like being fucked by a limb dude!" She wiggled her arm back and forth. "That shit's not normal."

"Yeah, he's got an abnormal penis." Nikki added.

I chuckled, a little.

"Come on now. How do you know he was really that big? He could have been lying." Stacey offered.

"You got pictures?" Nikki conspiratorially waggled her eyebrows.

"Yes. And NO, you can't see them!" I raised my voice for emphasis.

Nessa and Katie were looking at each other grinning.

"No! Absolutely not!" I said again but it was already too late. Nessa and Katie, normally at each other's throats, raced together for the stairs and the rest of the girls followed suit giggling the whole way. Taking my time, I climbed the stairs after them. I wasn't worried.

Ever since the impromptu visit from Adrian, I'd password protected my computer. They wouldn't get far. At least I hoped not.

My heart pounded. So much had passed between Seva and I in my bedroom. And now he hadn't contacted me in two months. Why not?

Strolling into the bedroom, I took in the scene. Nikki, Charlie, and Katie were sprawled out on my king size bed. Stacey was in the plush burgundy chair in the corner and Nessa was at my desk. I sat on the lambskin rug and asked innocently, "Find anything?"

"No. There's a freakin password," Nessa said dejectedly.

"Hmph!" was all I said. Reaching over to the desk, I grabbed my iPod off the desk and flipped to the pictures. The room remained quiet. I glanced up and noticed several interested stares.

"Hang on. You can pass it around ... " I held up my hand.

Scrolling to his pictures, there was only one where he was naked. It was the one from the bottom half of his stomach down, the one that showed off the lower half of his eight-pack abdomen and him in a deflated state. Looking at the picture I recalled how I had to stare at it for a while to see it, like my brain wouldn't or couldn't process the image correctly. I had teased him that it looked like a third leg. The screen just barely captured the end of his member. I decided not to say anything and to see if the girls noticed as I shuffled the images and handed off the iPod to Nessa.

They all crowded around the bed together so they could all see. I remained seated on the carpet, judging their reactions.

"Oh My God Mara! He's f'n hot and gorgeous!" Charlie exclaimed.

"I know," I said while trying to keep a tight reign on my emotions.

"Is he mixed? He's a cutie," Stacey added.

"Yeah. He's Puerto Rican and black. Black Latin as he refers to himself."

"Totally soppable," Katie agreed.

"What?" Charlie said, looking at Katie.

Katie explained. "You know how you have a good meal and you got gravy left on the plate. The gravy was so good that you don't want to leave it on the plate but you don't want to be a pig about it? So you take your bread and use it to sop up the rest of the gravy. That guy is totally soppable!"

Rolling her eyes at Katie, Nessa muttered, "Damn country bumpkin." Turning her attention to Stacey, Nessa said, "Dude, you need glasses. Cutie? No! This dude is hot, like model hot!" she exclaimed. "Like sinful hot," she continued with her voice dropping by octaves. "Mind if I take a crack at 'em Mara. Maybe he's into a sista. What did you say his name was anyway?" she said rubbing her chest.

Katie pushed Nessa's shoulder, Stacey smacked Nessa's hand, Charlie shook her head, and Nikki furrowed her eyebrows at Nessa. I laughed at my female versions of the stooges. I wasn't surprised at their reaction. We all had really good taste in men.

"His name is Seva and yeah dude, I mind," I told Nessa in my best good-natured voice.

Charlie considered me for a moment. Under her gaze, I couldn't maintain the pretense anymore and my smile faltered.

"Honey, give it time. Maybe he'll have a good explanation," Charlie said soothingly.

Looking down, nodding my head. "And what would be a good enough explanation to you?"

My bedroom was silent for moment. Then I looked up to watch Charlie.

She looked nonplussed for a minute. "I don't know ... An accident maybe."

"A sick family member," Nikki said.

"An impromptu business trip ... I mean really, it could happen," Katie offered.

"Yeah, you're right. But two months. That's a long time to go from communication every day multiple times in a day to nothing." I sighed.

"Yeah, it is," Charlie agreed.

"Yeah." Katie chimed in.

"I think you dodged a bullet if you asked me," Nessa said, her hands fisted on her hips.

A chorus of "Nobody asked you" rang through the room. We all burst out laughing. I felt a little better.

Stacey turned the iPod vertical then horizontal and looked at me with furrowed brows, "Is this what I think it is?" I gave her a huge smile and got several pillows thrown my way. It was so good to have friends.

I almost didn't need a lover, I lied to myself. Almost.

CHAPTER 8

I couldn't concentrate worth a damn. It was Monday afternoon and I was distracted, could barely hold a thought in my head. *Early dementia.* I had thought coffee would have solved it but not even that helped. I was so distracted that my coffee had gone unattended for so long that it was stone cold. Thank goodness for Katie. She had practically run Monday's morning meeting herself. I did little but make an occasional comment. It's like she just knew and I didn't have to explain. God love her, she was always there for me.

I knew what it was. I wanted to go home, lock the door and turn off the phone. I wanted to stare at nothing and do nothing. *How did my life turn out like this?* I was supposed to be married with 2.5 kids. Back that up. I was supposed to be married. Jury was still out on the kid thing. I got attached too fast, full steam ahead. I put my heart before my head and I knew better. And that was the truth of it, I did know better. I should have known better.

I'd been standing at the wide, nearly wall-sized window in my office, staring at the Mountain View cityscape just beyond my window, absently fingering the pearl necklace that complimented the black chiffon blouse and cream skirt I wore. This city was nothing like the cities in North Carolina. It was just gray, one building beside another with varying degrees of height. A definite concrete jungle. As much as I hated the country with the bugs and the heat, I loved the wide-open spaces and the sense of serenity that you just couldn't get in a big city.

"Penny for your thoughts?" a masculine voice asked.

"Hmmm, wha—" I said half-heartedly. I turned expecting to see Michael standing in the doorway and instead was shocked to see Eric DeVante lounging against the doorjamb. I recognized him from the last time we'd met briefly, some time in the previous year.

He looked every bit the executive, dressed as he was in a double-breasted gray suit. I was no fashionista but if I had to guess, I would say he was wearing an Armani suit. The man was seriously tall and I was short enough. I hated for someone to tower over me so I would usually give a really tall person some space or find a way to seat them quickly. Snapping back into professional mode with a shake to my head to try and clear the cobwebs I said, "Mr. DeVante! To what do I owe the pleasure of your company?"

"Eric please!" he answered.

"Right. Do come in? Would you like coffee, tea?" I said as I offered him a seat at the small conference table in front of the window.

The proverbial tall, dark, and handsome, Eric DeVante was sure to turn any woman's head. He had close-cropped hair that was slightly wavy, angular cheeks, a narrow nose, full lips, and striking green eyes.

"Coffee if you would. Black." He was glancing around my office as I called Michael's extension and asked him to bring in coffee. Grabbing my notebook and a pen, I settled into the seat opposite him and gave him my full attention.

"Nicely done, Ms. Simmons," he said nodding and looking around at my office.

"Thank you, but Amara, please." Michael knocked and I waived him in. As he settled the insulated carafe and disposable cups on the table, I noticed that my client was appreciating more than just the décor. Or was that my imagination? I took a moment to peek at his profile. The man was definitely easy on the eyes and he wore sex appeal like a second skin. But there was something about him that was just kinda ... off. I couldn't put my finger on it but something about him was amiss.

"A touch masculine, don't you think?" He waved perfectly manicured fingers toward my office the décor. I glanced at the room painted with stark white walls and furnished in shades of burgundy and browns.

"Perhaps ... I never noticed." I feigned innocence. Just because the room wasn't decorated in shades of pink and purple didn't mean a thing. It reminded me of home—everything except the stark white walls that I'd always been meaning to change. I had considered beige but every time I did I envisioned my wardrobe and imagined myself dressed in beige, in a beige painted room, with mostly shades of brown and it was just a little too ... beige.

"So ... " I began expectantly with raised eyebrows.

"I'd like to call in my chips, Ms. Simm- ... Amara," he corrected. He placed a closed Pendaflex file on the desk and slid it towards me.

"Would you care to elaborate, Eric?" I gestured to the file never touching it.

"I'd like you to go to Puerto Rico and mediate the situation for me. Of course, I expect you will close the deal."

Uh huh, of course. Out loud I said, "Why me? Surely you have got more than enough qualified staff on the payroll" I noticed him watching me carefully. "How many people have you already thrown at this thing? You're expecting me to accomplish something that you've surely had a team of people handling?"

He looked out the window for a moment and then returned my gaze. I shivered involuntarily at the intensity of it. "I've had a few lawyers look into to it in the hopes of finding legal loop holes. No such luck. For the most part I've tried to handle the situation on my own, unsuccessfully I might add. I do believe the situation could benefit from a woman's touch."

There was something else there, something he wasn't telling me. My stomach jumped. "When do you need my answer?" I asked, stalling for time. "I could look over the file and get back to you ... "

"I need an answer today. Although I've asked politely, let there be no misconception. I expect you to be on the plane tomorrow."

I could feel the heat creeping into my cheeks as I struggled to maintain my composure and control my escalating temper. *Ah, mystery revealed. The charmer was an act. The man was really a prick.* I looked out the window, swinging my pen back and forth between my fingers, watching him out of the corner of my eye. He was watching me the whole time, sipping his coffee, waiting. *Why should I?* He could find someone else. He had enough money to do it. I hated to be bullied and he was definitely a bully.

I looked over at him with half a mind to tell him thanks but no thanks when I considered who I was dealing with and looked out the window again. He had too many contacts that I needed, many more friends and associates with which he could easily taint my company's reputation. This was a win-win for him. He didn't have to pay me. The contracts were set. I couldn't demand any more money. *Dude's got me by the short and curlies and he knows it. Prick, prick, prick, prick!* I ranted mentally. I had made my little "prick" mantra into a song of sorts in my head and I was nodding slightly at each one. Then I realized that I was in public, in front of my client, and I took up the nervous habit of swinging my pen back and forth again. I said nothing, waiting for something better.

Clearing his throat, he brought my attention back to him. "You must be thinking, 'What's in it for me?' " I didn't answer, just raised one eyebrow, crossing my legs and lacing my hands in my lap.

He continued. "Let's make our relationship exclusive— our business relationship. You handle all of my real estate matters including residential and commercial properties. I dump and pick up property all the time," he said with a casual wave of a hand.

Yeah, multi million dollar properties. That was better. I gazed out the window again. It was a good offer, solid even, but I thought that he was leaving things out and I hated to commit to something if I didn't really know what I was getting into. I waited some more.

"Still the question 'eh? Why you?" Eric said with a smirk.

I nodded.

"I'm in the habit of employing either sharks or mice. You are neither. You are a wolf dressed as a lamb, Amara. I believe this could be a skill that would be most advantageous in this situation."

"Hmph," was all I had to say to that.

"I was rude earlier. I should apologize," he offered.

It wasn't lost on me at all that saying one should apologize and doing it were two entirely different things.

I took a deep breath. "Give me a run down of the situation. What exactly am I in for?"

He shrugged, then smiled in a wolfish grin. "I'm trying to buy property. They keep putting up roadblocks. It's pretty simple."

I decided I was all in and called his bluff. "Bullshit."

Chuckling, he said, "Ah, there's a woman with some fire. Okay. I'll be straight with you. The property I want to build is pretty great. I need buy a sizeable acreage for it to one, be worth my while, and two, for me to be able to accommodate all the amenities that I want to offer to exclusive clientele. However, there is some ridiculous argument about environmental impact and endangered species. The neighbors are a bunch of pansy asses and the zoning officials are dick wads." He sat back in the chair, apparently finished with his tirade.

"Is dick wad an official term? Can I quote you on that?" I said with a grin. I was starting to warm up to him.

"Yeah, I know. I have colorful language."

Laughing out loud I said, "Oh, you've got nothing on my girlfriends." I sobered and looked at him in the eyes. "So just how hard have you made my job, Eric?"

He got up and walked to the wastebasket on the other side of the room and threw his cup in the garbage. He slid his hands in his pockets and turned toward me. "The negotiator—a Mr. Vittorio—we don't seem to see eye to eye on a few key points."

"Just a few or all?" I raised an eyebrow and gave him a sardonic grin.

"Touché," he said rocking on his heels. "So you'll go?"

I tilted my head to the side and looked at him. His good looks weren't lost on me. In fact, if I wasn't in my professional mode, I might let myself feel the attraction to him that seemed to simmer beneath the surface. It had been too long since I'd been with a man. I ignored the low hum in my core and turned back to business. "Can I take you at your word? Can I trust this little caveat that you've used to entice my cooperation is to be honored once this deal is done?"

"I give you my word, Ms. Simmons, and I never go back on my word. I will hold up my end of this bargain so long as you fulfill yours. Close the deal and we're in business." His piercing pale green eyes gazed into mine. For a moment I was caught.

Then I broke the spell and went to my desk. I looked up at him and nodded, then called Katie on the intercom.

She strode in with a smile on her face. Today she looked like a lovely tulip in a yellow blouse and olive green pants and olive colored pumps.

"This is our client, Eric DeVante." I introduced them.

"Katie," Eric said shaking her hand.

"Mr. DeVante. Nice to finally put a face to the paperwork," Katie joked.

"Katie, I will be out of town starting tomorrow and will be gone for the next—" I looked at Eric for confirmation.

"At least a week," he answered.

"A week?!" I asked turning to him with wide eyes.

"Or less," he shrugged. *Prick*. How could a handsome man be such a prick? Why did it seem like they all were?

I turned back to Katie. "A week. Think you can hold down the fort?"

She turned and walked to the door, calling over her shoulder, "I think I can manage. Ya'll have fun, you hear."

I was still looking at the door shaking my head when Eric said, "I'm not going with you."

"Excuse me?"

"I have another engagement to attend to so you're on your own tomorrow." He pulled out his blackberry and typed in a text message. He looked back up at me and spoke brusquely. "Well, I believe that's everything. My driver will be by your place in the morning to pick you up, 7am sharp. He'll take you to the airport where you will take my private jet directly to Puerto Rico." He started walking to the door, glancing down at his watch. "It's hot there. Really hot." Turning around he glanced down at me. "Be sure to take sun block. With your pale skin, you wouldn't want to burn."

"Just a minute," I called out. He was standing there with his hand on the doorknob and turned back to face me. "This wolf has one more thing to add."

A look of surprise passed through his eyes, but recovered quickly, waiting for me to speak, a look of impatience on his face.

"Anything goes." I stepped up to him and looked up, my arms crossed over my chest.

"Pardon me?" he asked.

"You're sending me into the lion's den, alone. You're giving me a night to get myself acclimated with the nuances of the conflict and to be able to work out a solution. On top of that, you've put the success of a business deal that should have closed months ago along with potential future endeavors, all hinging on a deal you couldn't close yourself. So what do you do? You leave it up to some lackey to do it for you."

He said nothing, but his expression changed from impatient to pissed.

I held up my hand in a stop gesture. I had more to say. "I, Mr. DeVante, am no lackey. So ... anything goes." I held out my hand to him for him to shake.

He narrowed his eyes at me and considered my outstretched hand.

Stupid, stupid. You've gone too far. Should have just kept my mouth shut. But I held firm and didn't flinch.

He nodded once. "Agreed," he said and shook my hand. "Try not to buy the island on my behalf, okay," he joked.

"Oh, of course not. That would be silly," I said in my best flippant manner.

I watched him leave, a handsome man in a confusing tightly wound package, and walked over to my desk and called Michael's extension. "Michael, I need to ask for a favor." Silence. "Michael?" I said slightly irritated.

"Oh yes ma'am. I'm here. You've never asked me for anything. Not like a favor kind of thing. I mean I—"

"Michael" I interrupted. "I need you to do some digging. Now. First I need background on Puerto Rico. Anything you think would be pertinent. What's the culture like? Am I gonna need a translator? What's the political climate like? How do they view the US? That kind of thing. I need a peek into their psyche, if you will. Send me an email with the most important things listed and then attach all the background if you would. I need it by 8pm. You think you can handle that?"

"Absolutely!" he answered excitedly.

"Oh, and one more thing. I want you to do some digging on our client. There's something he's not telling me. My gut says he's got some connection to this thing more than what he's telling."

"That's gonna take longer than four hours," he said.

"I know but it's necessary."

"I'll see what I can come up with."

"Thank you." I hung up, grabbed my purse, and jammed the file DeVante had given me into my briefcase.

"Going shopping?" Katie asked standing in the doorway.

"How much did you hear?" I asked glancing around for my keys.

Katie walked into my office and grabbed my jacket off the back of my desk chair, patting the pockets and coming up with the keys. "Something about some animals, you not being anybody's lackey and you commandeering my assistant."

Grinning, I said, "All that huh? It's a wonder he didn't walk into you when he stepped out in the hallway." She shrugged. "Yes, I'm going shopping but just because I've never been to the islands. I don't have that gauzy island stuff in my closet."

"You mean linen?" Katie suggested.

"Yeah, that stuff. I want to fit in and be comfortable." I stuffed my arms into my jacket.

"It's a good thing summer clothes are still out here this late into the season," she added.

"Yeah, I guess so." I wasn't sure if I could do it. I had a lot riding on this it. Could I really do it all? I looked at her for a second.

She came up to me and hugged me and whispered, "You'll do fine. Trust yourself."

CHAPTER 9

As the plane landed in sunny Puerto Rico morning, I was still so irritated with Eric DeVante I could have used his face as a punching bag. The driver had called to inform me that he'd be picking me up at 11 pm, not 7am the next morning. So instead of getting a decent night's sleep, I got none. The nonstop flight from San Francisco had been a sleepless eight-hour long journey.

I was grateful for my impromptu shopping spree as I stepped off the plane onto the tarmac. It was indeed hot. Weather reports had said it would be about 80 degrees, humidity at 86 percent. It felt like it was 95 degrees outside. Although it was completely different from home—sand instead of red clay dirt, aqua marine oceans instead of the muddy brown of the Atlantic Ocean, it reminded me of humid summers back home in North Carolina. I took a deep breath and let the morning sun warm my up-stretched face. I had never been outside the continental United States.

From where I stood I could see that the island was positively beautiful. The skies were so blue that the blue green oceans seemed to reflect their image. I had seen pictures, even saw video online, but the beauty of the islands definitely was meant to be experienced and not observed from a distance. I sighed and thought of all I read during the flight.

I'd spent most of my hours awake on the private jet going over the material Michael had emailed me. Stateside textbooks had glossed over the history of how the island came to be a US territory. In 1940s, the US just basically invaded and took possession of the island. They made everyone a citizen whether they wanted to be one or not. To this day, half the inhabitants of the island chafed under US rule and the other half courted it. The island was dependent on the US for more than half its exports and it also had the highest unemployment rate compared to any state in the US. Private sector jobs and development were low and was among the many criticisms critics on the island accused the government of. The atrocities went on. Although Puerto Ricans were US citizens, taxed like the rest of us on the mainland, paying for social security and Medicare like the rest of us blokes, they couldn't vote in national elections. They had no actual say in the government that had been forced down their throats years ago. It seems that the US had attempted several times to right their wrongs by giving Puerto Rico the chance to seek to become a state. Each time, Puerto Rico had withdrawn their application, never being united in their quest.

It was valuable information to have. I suspected that if all the people involved in these negotiations were native, they were likely to be divided probably right down the middle. There would be some that wanted to see the deal happen and others that would see it as another wealthy American trying to usurp the natural wealth of the island.

We had flown directly into the Culebra airport. The same city that the US had established a naval base on oh so long ago and had only closed in the last twenty years. Though the airport usually serviced smaller planes, they had permitted the wealthy Americans access, like Eric DeVante. I squinted against the sun and saw the limo idling with the driver standing by the car, waiting to usher me inside.

As I walked toward the black car, exhaustion pressed against me. I had a healthy fear of heights and it didn't matter if travel by plane was one of the most secure forms of transportation. I could still go hurtling to my death from hundreds of feet from the sky. Didn't matter that I'd been on a luxurious private jet as the only passenger.

I slid into the car, grateful for the cool feel of the red leather seats. Every piece of clothing felt like it was glued to me. I tried to fluff my blouse away from my body to cool off. I had it extended and was blowing down the V-necked front when I heard a throat being cleared. I froze and lowered my blouse. Blinded by the glare from the sun streaming in from the sunroof, I slid back into the darkened corner to see better and realized that I was not alone.

"Uh, hello," I said hesitantly. I couldn't see him quite clearly except to see he was wearing a dark double-breasted suit.

"Ms. Simmons, I presume."

Creepy much, I thought. "So, I see my reputation precedes me. And you are?" I prompted.

"Pleased to meet you," the man answered sitting forward so that the sunlight cast light to one side of his face and kept the other half in shadow. I was just waiting for him to sound like Count Dracula, shrouded in shadow as he was and say in a Transylvanian accent, "I am here to drink your blood." Instead he extended his hand for me to grasp. "You can call me Rey." His voice was smooth with a courteous rumble and Latin accent.

I scooted forward and shook his hand. "Hello Rey. And to what do I owe the pleasure of your acquaintance?"

"Eric called and asked if I minded escorting a beauty around the island. I must admit that I was curious to see if you were as cute as he claimed you to be. I dare say that his description was not accurate enough. I'll have to talk to him about that," he said with a half-smirk. I couldn't tell if it was a whole smirk. I still couldn't see his whole face.

"Thank you!" I was determined to appear cool and collected despite the fact that I felt frumpy and ruffled. "Are you familiar with the terms of this business deal?"

"Loosely," he said with a slight wave of his hand. "I have warned Eric but he can be so head strong," he added with a tsk. "The area he wants to build in is a zoned-for-residential use only. It was zoned that way because the US government used to test weapons there. Environmentalists argue about the impact to the environment, the sea turtles. They are an endangered species. This is no small thing, mind you, but Eric can be relentless when he wants something. He doesn't like to be challenged." He looked at me pointedly and said, "And he doesn't like to be told no."

I crossed my arms and legs and leaned forward. I nodded. "Somehow ... I got that impression! So how do you know Mr. DeVante? Are you business associates?"

I had forgotten when I leaned forward about the type of blouse I had on and how much cleavage it showed. However, I was reminded when he broke eye contact and gazed appreciatively at my bosom. Ordinarily, I would have slid back, re-adjusted my blouse, tucked my skirt around me and tried to cover my knees too. But today, I was ready to be a little bold. *Why the hell not. I'm single. Not like Seva gives a damn.* When he made eye contact again, I raised an eyebrow and gave him a slight smile.

He slid forward, his face no longer in shadow and propped up my chin with his finger. "Maldita sea. Eres bien seductora. Te nace naturalmente," he whispered.

Whatever he said, it sounded sexy. I caught that it was something about seduction or something natural.

He was so close that I could feel his breath on my face. His face was no longer in shadow. He was light in complexion, thick eyebrows, broad nose, pearl white teeth, wide mouth, and brown eyes. His slicked back hair curled up at the ends around his face. While he was easy on the eyes, I felt nothing. Not even the slightest twinge. He slid back to the shadows in the corner and angled his body away from me, crossing his legs.

He smoothed imaginary wrinkles on his pants leg with his hand. "Eric and I are friends. I forget how many years but quite a few, since we children."

"Are you a native of Puerto Rico?"

"Eric and I both are, although you wouldn't know it to look at him. He passes for white so easily. His mother was Puerto Rican but his father was from California. The rest is a story that Eric must tell. It is not my tale to tell. Let's just suffice it to say that Eric was motivated to make something of himself. He did better than most and more than expected. I'm proud of him. I don't know that it means much to him, though."

"Hmmm," was all I said. What a small world. Who would have guessed that Eric and I shared mixed heritage. "So, what do you do for a living, if I may ask?"

"Let's just say that I deal in imports and exports."

"Ahhh. I see." *Drugs.*

"I'm sure you do, querida. I would like for you to join me for dinner. I can take you out on my boat later. if you like. It's warm here on the island, even at night."

I said nothing as the car came to a stop outside the hotel.

Rey continued. "You will have plenty of time to refresh yourself. Your meeting will be held here in the hotel at 2pm this afternoon. Any cost, please put it on the room. Eric will take care of everything. I will be happy to take you on a tour of the island. I will call on you at seven for dinner."

As if on cue, the driver opened the door and so it seemed, I had been dismissed.

As I exited the car I turned back and said, "Thank you for the welcome."

He leaned forward and looked me directly in the eyes right before the driver shut the door. "The pleasure, I hope, will be all mine, Ms. Simmons."

CHAPTER 10

Islands, sun, beach. And work. Somehow, those things just didn't seem to go together. I had checked in and been escorted to a private bungalow right on the beach. It was absolutely stunning. The beach was just a few feet from my doorstep. I kept expecting the worse and was rewarded with the best money could buy. I don't know why but I expected a shack with a rickety fan. I expected it to be sweltering. It was neither. My first apartment hadn't been this big. The room was decorated in ocean blue and trimmed in white. Shrouded in a curtain draped from the ceiling, the bed was king sized, dressed in pristine ironed white sheets, and the focal point of the room as it was perched atop a three step square landing. I looked around and uttered a very impressed, "Ah!" Then I called Katie to check in on the office.

"Excellent Realty. Katie speaking," she answered primly.

"Well it must be jelly cause jam don't shake like that!"

She paused a moment and bust out laughing. "Said the pot to the kettle. How is sunny Puerto Rico? It is sunny, right?"

"Oh yes ma'am. That and then some."

"So tell me, did that fine ass Eric DeVante take care of you?"

"You know this morning, I could have spit nails I was so irritated with him at the moved up departure. But I have to say, he has redeemed himself. This place is awesome. Now,

I'm probably giving him a whole lot more allowances than he deserves but somehow, the Jacuzzi tub, fully stocked kitchen with an island, and central AC seems to have made up for his oversight last night."

"Oh, nah uh. You get to go to Puerto Rico for a business trip and you get pampered while I'm stuck here, like a slave, working my po' fingers to the bone. Now, that just ain't right I tell ya. It just ain't," Katie said in her fake drama voice.

I could just see her holding the phone between her shoulder and ear and using finger quotation marks when she said "business trip."

"Aw … poor baby. You know I'm gonna do right by you. Don't you worry you pretty little head about it."

"Uh huh … I've heard that before! So when do you duke it out with the locals?"

"This afternoon."

"Are you nervous?"

"Nope."

"Okay. That means yes."

"Yep. That means nope."

"I'm gonna get off da phone and get back to a little thing called work. You know … the thing we peons are expected to do before you confuse the hell outta me."

I laughed. "Whatever!"

"Call me later. I'd like to know just how hot the Latino men are."

"I can tell you already. Hot. And pretty … very easy on the eyes."

"K. I gotta run but seriously, do everything, stress on the *everything*, Nessa and I both would do."

"Bye fool."

"Enjoy yourself girl! The beach is calling." Katie clicked off.

I hung up the phone and laid back. The curtains were parted at the end of the bed and patio doors open. I had a clear view of the beach right from the bed and it was fabulous. I imagined it was beautiful at night. That made me think back to one of the last instant message exchanges that Seva and I had. I was asking him about his home country. I'd typed:

> Me: How often do you go back to Puerto Rico? Do you have family there?

> Sevastien: I do have family there. My parents and brother relocated to the States when I was five but my grandmother is still in Puerto Rico. She cooks the best Lechón. Can you cook baby?

> Me: I have been known to cook a thing or two.

> Sevastien: Hmmm. I can't wait. You know what else I can't wait to do? I can't wait to lick you. Would you like that baby? Would you like me to lick that pretty kitty?

> Me: Oh yeah. You know you got to put in work if I'm expected to fit all that you got going on south of the border.

> Sevastien: You know. I really can't imagine why someone hasn't scooped you up. You are funny, so funny. And real. Like you know, you tell it kinda just ... straight.

> Me: I don't know any other way to be than just me. You either like it or lump it as the saying goes.

> Sevastien: Oh, I'd like to take it over and over and over and over again.

> Me: Promises, promises. What would be your version of a perfect night for us?

> Sevastien: Hmmm. OK. Picture this. We make dinner together. A bunch of stolen

kisses, caresses, an occasional grope here and there. I would be the one doing the groping by the way.

Me: Don't count on it.

Sevastien: When dinner is over, we go for a walk on the beach. The night is still warm and the moon is high. I undress you and we go for a swim together, naked. In the ocean. We kiss. Hot and heavy. You would look so hot. Skin glistening. Bathed in moonlight. Your nipples peeking just above the water. Perky and hard. I slide deep inside your body, fucking you slow. Building in momentum. Watching your face glow in the night. I want that. I want all of that.

I woke up two hours later with my hands fisted in the sheets.

I got up and took a shower. I ordered room service and had a light lunch of cut fruit and salad. The breeze was coming in from the ocean so I decided to sit out on the patio and review the DeVante file.

The main problems with the deal were that the area that DeVante wanted was indeed strictly zoned for residential use. Then there was the turtle problem that I was very sure my client could care less about. Community leaders for the area wanted to keep noise levels, traffic, and commercialization to a minimum. Larger issues seemed to have impacted the deal as well. Unemployment was higher here than it was in any one state in the US. On top of that, college graduates faced stiff competition for jobs due to the lack of job creation. Admittedly, the deck was stacked. I had a few ideas but I decided my strategy initially would be just to watch. I had no delusions of grandeur. As if they were all just waiting for me to come in and save the day. My guess was it would be a bit of an uphill battle.

I had bought a large straw purse that would double as a briefcase so I could easily blend in. That afternoon I prepared for the meeting carefully. I slipped on my new beige linen pants suit with wedges in place of heels. I used minimal makeup to appear as non confrontational as possible. I just used mascara to highlight my eyes and nearly nude lip gloss. I gave myself a once over before walking over to the hotel. I had color to my cheeks and despite my lack of sleep, I looked alert. More importantly, I looked unsuspecting. All apart of my plan I thought to myself. "Let's get this show on the road" I said out loud to the balmy Puerto Rican air as I crossed the hotel lobby.

I walked over the front desk to have a porter escort me to a large conference room. I was actually a little early but it appeared as though the meeting was already under way. Discreetly, the porter allowed me to slip into the back of the room. There was a buffet set up there with hors d'oeuvres, cut fruit, and cut vegetables. I knew from the last meeting minutes that had been in the file that there were zoning officials, urban planners, representatives of the homeowners community, student protesters from the UDP, environmentalists and the sellers liaison, a Mr. Vittorio.

An older gentleman approached me and introduced himself. I recognized his name as being one of the lawyers associated with the deal. I introduced myself and he led me to the only available seat in the room, just left of the head of the table. I took out my leather bound portfolio and laid it on the table and placed my straw purse on the floor just left of my chair. Standing near the table was a younger man with his back to me dressed in a breezy gray shirt with black slacks.

The lawyer smiled at me and spoke in a kind voice, gesturing the younger man, "It was so good of you to come on short notice, Ms. Simmons. Let me introduce you to Mr. Vittorio. Mr. Sevastien Vittorio. He knows the ins and outs of this deal intimately."

My heart sped up. Could it be? No. Probably a coincidence.

I had a smile prepared as I turned around, and prepared to stick my hand out in greeting. But I was totally unprepared for the hand that encapsulated my own or the lips that kissed my hand or the deep baritone voice that said,

"It's nice to me you. Amara."

CHAPTER 11

No fucking way. It was Seva. In the flesh. This whole time he'd been the one who'd been holding up the DeVante deal. I thought back to his profile, "I'm a financial consultant." *This is soo not happening.*

We were staring at one another. God, he looked exactly like his pictures but he looked so much better in person. I never broke eye contact but I was tugging slightly at my hand. He was holding my hand, caressing the back of it, stroking it back and forth with his thumb. I was convinced I was daydreaming. Just a few hours ago I was fantasizing, dreaming about the man that promised to test the heights of any orgasm I had ever had and here he was in the flesh.

I could touch him.

Hell, I was touching him ... and he was touching me.

It felt so much better than any fantasy and he was only touching me hand.

"I ... " I stopped and glanced around quickly. People were starting to pay attention to the fact that we were taking a long time to be introduced to one another. I seemed to have a million and one questions. But we weren't alone and my questions would have to wait. I tugged a little more sharply and kept my eyes pointedly fixed on his chest.

He brought my hand slowly to his lips but held off on kissing my hand until I looked up at him. When I made eye contact, he kissed my hand and allowed me to take my hand away. "I'm glad you're here."

I glanced back up at him and gave him a curt nod as I turned back to my seat. I was trembling as I sat down in my seat, thankful I had worn my hair down so I could hid behind it as I rubbed my hand against my slacks where he had kissed it. I could still feel the imprint of his lips. I didn't need a mirror to see whether I was blushing. I was hot all over. My face felt like it was as red as a beet. I glanced up to examine the room for exits, but there was one way in and out.

I would have to pass by all those people on the way out. Not only that, but I very likely was going to have to stare Seva in the face as I walked back to the front of the room. I was trapped. My stomach was in a knot of nerves. I couldn't breathe. How was I going to do this? I didn't know whether to laugh or shout, be excited or angry. My heart beat like a scared rabbit's.

He sat down at the head of the table and had his head bent down as if he was studying the document he was holding. He said low enough that only I could hear. "We need to talk."

And that voice. There was no hint of an accent whatsoever ... just pure sexuality. How many times had I wondered and imagined what he would sound like? My imaginings were poor imitations of the real thing. He really *could* talk my drawers off. I opened my portfolio and wrote mundane inconsequential things like the date, Hotel Culebra, anything to try and keep my attention away from him. I just needed to do something with my hands.

"Seems like you could have done that anytime in the last two months," I said snidely under my breath. I had to get a hold of myself. I kept writing repeatedly, "You are a professional." Damn straight. I squared my shoulders, settled back into the chair, and gave him the coolest stare I could muster.

The afternoon crawled. This was the longest meeting I had ever been in. The presentation began with a film clip of the naval base that was now closed, drills that had involved weapons testing, a filmed report of the impact to aqua marine life in the area, and films of student protesters. Seva was directing the slides one by one, narrating along the way, from the corner of the room. Although I was trying hard not to look at him, I seemed to find him without trying anywhere he was in the room. I could feel the weight of his stare.

The next part of the presentation went to bulleted lists of statistical information. I had trouble concentrating. Just hearing his voice brought back all the sexy conversations we had in stark detail. Thankfully enough I had made early notes about potential compromise on the business deal so that I didn't need to track every little detail he was droning on about.

I was bent over my note pad writing out a business case analysis of pros and cons when I heard Seva call my name. I paused for a second, not certain if I had heard correctly, and heard him call my name again. I stopped writing and looked to my right and most everyone was looking at me. I dropped my pen and sat back, "Sorry. Yes?"

"Do you have any questions on the complexities of the situation so far?"

I glanced around the room and then back at him. "Have all nuances of the deal been presented thus far, Mr. Vittorio?" I saw a muscle tick in his jaw. I laced my fingers together over my abdomen and raised a questioning eyebrow at him.

"Pretty much. The last issue being that the seller is close to being in default on the taxes for the property, as he can no longer afford them. The deadline for default is at the end of the week," Seva said in an even voice.

Even better, I thought. I gestured to the white board and said to Seva coolly, "May I?"

"By all means." He handed me a marker for the board. As he placed the marker in my hand his fingertips brushed my palm. Heat shot through my body and I shivered in response. I pushed aside my desires and gave my attention to the white board.

I took a deep breath. *Here we go.* I laid it out point by point acknowledging all issues from local to political, environmental to national. I listed on one side of the board all issues against the DeVante deal. On the other side of the board I listed initial benefits to the DeVante deal including job creation, tourism, tax revenue. I turned to the room. "There are a few givens to be expected, yes?"

I looked around the room and caught a lot of nodding heads in agreement. I glanced at Sevastien who seemed to be genuinely interested in what I had to say. "So let's be realistic, shall we people?" I was starting to get into my groove and finally started to relax.

"First of all, let me say that not only am I here on Mr. DeVante's behalf but I am also authorized to negotiate the deal and sign on the dotted line. He's one wealthy American but he is also a native son. Even if he could offer jobs, just how many jobs could he offer? What kind of impact could be worth it to you?"

I heard a few numbers thrown out. Twenty thousand. Thirty-five thousand. I let that go on for a little while. Then they started debating amongst themselves that quickly became an argument among the student protesters and zoning officials. I knocked on the white board for order.

When I had their full attention, I said, "Ten percent. Let's say he could reduce unemployment by ten percent. What number does that translate to?" I looked around the room. "Anyone?"

Seva said, "Sixty thousand."

I smiled and dove right in with my proposal. "That's right. Thank you, Sevastien. Sixty thousand jobs. Manufacturing rates in Puerto Rico are the lowest among US states and territories with nearly a four to one ratio. So, I'm talking about boosting private sector investment, job creation from construction to manufacturing to education."

Some of the men in the room started nodding. I kept going.

"We are willing to have an environmental impact study done and to engage in open discussions about the best way to have minimal impact on the environment. We're willing to make a commitment to conservation and to work with urban planners to reduce noise and traffic congestion issues for local residents."

"No way," someone shouted from the back of the room. "He can't possibly do all that." Came another.

"I promise you, it can be done. A native son, giving back to his home country. You would deny him this? You would deny yourselves?" I said with my hand on hip. I looked solidly at every person seated at the table. I was really convinced this was the best solution for everybody. They all started murmuring amongst themselves. I looked at Seva. He was sitting with his ankle resting on his knee, considering me.

I stepped up to him and said loud enough for everyone to hear, "I trust you will handle the settlement of the details and send a yea or nay back to my client."

He stood and guided me by the elbow to the corner of the room away from prying ears. "You and I both know that what you've suggested here today is a win-win situation for all. Including my client. Beautiful and smart," he said and trailed a finger down the side of my face. "Have dinner with me," he whispered.

Inside I was screaming, "Yes. Absolutely yes. Now!" Aloud I said, "I'll have to take a rain check. I have a date that I have to get ready for. I believe we'll be dining here for the night. Perhaps I'll see you around."

"Amara ... " he pleaded softly, his eyes yearning and open.

"Perhaps this form of communication is too forward for you. Excuse me. I wouldn't want to be late." I went to step around him and he blocked my path.

"We need to talk," he said through clenched teeth, softness gone and replaced by a hard tone.

His body was blocking mine from the rest of the room. I reached out and touched his chest. I leaned into him and stood on tippy toe to reach his ear and whispered sarcastically, "Send me an email."

CHAPTER 12

The night was breezy but humid. As promised, Rey, DeVante's friend, showed up at my door promptly at 7pm. He was dressed classy but casual in a white linen button down shirt and pants with closed toe loafers. I was dressed for the occasion in a strapless turquoise cotton dress with a split straight up the front of the dress from mid calf to mid thigh. I set the outfit off with a pair of black strappy sandals.

I'd marched straight to the hotel's boutique shop and bought this little island number right after I left Sevastien in the conference room. I tried on the outfit and smiled appreciatively into the mirror. "This'll do." I wanted to make the bastard as hot for me as I had been for him ... as I still was for him.

Except the dress had worked a little too well if Rey's reaction had been anything to go by.

I'd had the wrap in hand when Rey knocked and I'd opened the door.

As he looked me up and down his eyes widened with appreciation.

"Well hello there! I see you're punctual." I grabbed my silver clutch purse and draped a sheer turquoise cover with a shimmered fringe across my chest.

He gazed at me from the doorway. "And you are stunning!"

I blushed, feeling the flush on my cheeks. "Thank you!"

We'd made our way to the hotel dining room and ordered dinner. Rey made polite conversation, asking me how I'd met Eric and about my business. I was distracted the whole time while we ate. I kept glancing around the room for Seva but there was no sign of him. Rey asked me how the meeting had gone and I glossed over the details. I just told him that it had gone well and the deal looked promising.

Perhaps I should have been more receptive to Seva. Maybe I should have given him the time to talk to me. We had at least been in the same space, same time zone.

After dinner, Rey led me out to the patio, placing his hand in the small of my back to guide me. He held the door open for me and left just enough room for me to slip through. Just enough room for my body to graze against his own.

Several things had happened on this night that were not my imagination. Every time Rey guided me to a table or through a doorway, his hand managed to slip a little lower than waist level or his hand would brush my bottom. It was never enough for me to openly take issue with but it was more than enough to set my teeth on edge. So it didn't improve my mood whatsoever when I squeezed by him and discovered he was more than a little happy to see me. I was damn near salivating for an argument. It was either that or some other hot and sweaty sexual activity. I would love to take the latter ... just not with this guy. So I bit my tongue.

Rey had been a fine host, very pleasant, gracious at carrying most of the conversation. The man was obviously attractive and considering the stares, or daggers, that had been directed my way, nearly any unattached and seemingly attached woman would have gladly traded places with me. I leaned my hips against the railing and spread my hands alongside it staring at the moonlit beach.

I was hyperaware that Rey was watching me in profile.

"I trust I have been a sufficient host this evening?" he asked.

I glanced up at him quickly and gave him a half smile, returning my gaze to the beach. "Indeed."

"Do you find my company to be unpleasant, Amara? Is that it?"

I raised an eyebrow, still looking at the ocean waves lap calmly upon the private beach and asked absentmindedly without looking at him, "Why ever would you think such a thing?"

"Clearly, I do not rank high among your thoughts. You have been distracted all night. I would hope to be the man to be the center of your attention, but clearly I am not. Perhaps I should take my leave of you?"

I turned to him fully prepared to offer some lame excuse about a situation at home, or that I was worried about DeVante's reaction but instead I turned around instinctively and looked just past Rey to the man standing in his shadow.

My heart sped up. He looked fantastic. Even in the glow of the moon I could tell he was dressed in a light orange button down shirt open just past mid chest with dark slacks. He looked gorgeous! My body already anticipating his.

"Perhaps you should," Seva said in a deep voice with just a hint of menace.

Rey turned around and looked at Seva, a curious open look on his face.

"Allow me to introduce myself. My name is Sevastien Vittorio. And you are?"

"Salvatore Reyes," Rey said as he shook Seva's hand.

Rey turned back to me, no doubt about to ask me if I knew the uninvited party, when I noticed he noticed my state of arousal. I just watched Seva. I didn't say a word. I knew he could see my nipples hard and eager. I opened my mouth but didn't make a sound. What could I say? Seva watched me the whole time. I kept glancing from him to Rey. Oh boy! Why did I feel guilty? I hadn't done anything wrong but I felt guilty nevertheless.

"Rey ..." I started.

Rey looked at me and smiled, ever the gracious man. He took my hand and kissed it. "Thank you for having dinner with me. I trust I leave you in good hands?"

That and then some. But I still couldn't find my voice.

"I promise to take good care of her," Seva said staring at me, menace still in his voice.

"Make sure you do, hombre." Rey waited until Seva broke eye contact with me to give him a curt nod. Then Rey nodded at me and returned to the dining room.

"I leave you alone for a few hours and you're hanging out with drug dealers?" Seva took a step toward me.

My breath came short. I managed to finally speak. "I recall he phrased it as imports and exports."

He closed the last few steps between us and leaned the side of his hip against the railing, barely a foot between us. He gazed down at me. "Ahhh," was all he said.

"You look exactly like your picture," I whispered.

"As do you."

God, how long, how often had I imagined this moment? I wanted so much to touch him. But I held back. I was still a little angry at him.

"Do you remember the night we talked about a moon lit beach?" he said seductively. He reached out and took my hand, and I let him. He rubbed his thumb back and forth across the back of my hand.

Do I ever? I haven't been able to forget since I got here. "Maybe. Refresh my memory." I leaned into him.

CHAPTER 13

"Would you like a glass of wine?" Seva asked. We were in his house just a mile down the beach from my hotel. We had walked down the beach to his house hand in hand. I was nervous. I'd glanced at my hand in his own. Such large hands that encompassed my own completely. I so wanted those hands to touch me, to cover and caress my body.

"White or red?" Seva asked standing at the galley of his kitchen leaning against the wall. He was sexual chocolate personified, looking at me from head to toe with his hands in his pockets. The man never looked sexier. I wanted to run my hands down the inside of shirt to touch his exposed chest. Matter of fact ... I wanted it off all together. My hands actually itched.

I licked my lips and cleared my throat and I answered hoarsely. "Red." I glanced around the living room. The room was decorated in pale yellow walls with a large white sectional in the middle of the room. I slipped the wrap from my shoulders and laid it on the sofa. I felt him behind me and smelled his cologne before I saw him. My skin heated and my heart beat faster; wine forgotten.

He trailed a finger down my arm. I was still facing away from him.

"Baby girl," he whispered.

I closed my eyes, parted my lips and blew out a breath. His voice was so deep in timbre. It resonated through my body. He used both hands and ran his hands through my hair gently and smoothed my hair back.

He bent down and nuzzled my neck. "You smell so good." He stepped close to me and I could feel the hardness of his body against mine. He fisted his hands in my hair and snapped my head back at an angle and swallowed my moan in a kiss. Lips so soft, so full. He slipped his hand around me, his hand flat against my stomach. Just under my breasts. Molding my body to his own. He ground his hips against me and I could feel him rock hard behind me. He grunted as I ground my hips against him. I broke the kiss and turned around to face him.

He looked like he was just barely holding himself in check. His jaw was tight with desire. It had been forever since a man had looked at me like this. A man that I could touch, freely. Need so clearly written on his face. I wanted to go fast and I wanted to go slow. I wanted to draw this out but I wanted to feel my naked body against his. Now.

He reached out and held my neck underneath my hair and drew me to him. He was holding my head angled up to him with both thumbs stroking my cheeks back and forth. "Give me this night baby. Give us tonight."

I caressed his chest, soft downy hair and hard muscles, warm and vibrant.

He kissed me softly on the lips. "Say yes, baby." He rested his forehead against my mine and whispered, "Please. Say yes."

I had one hand on his waist and the other trailing down his arm to his hand and back down again. *If I can only have one night, then I'll make the most of it.*

I lifted my head and whispered back, "Yes."

I drew back and looked at him. He blew out a breath and gave me the sexiest smile. That smile held a lot of promise, one I hoped he would keep well into the night. He scooped me up in his arms, kissing me as if I was the most delicious thing he'd ever tasted, and lazily as if we had all the time in the world. We kissed as he walked up the stairs with me in his arms. And in those fifteen steps I discovered that he was playful too when he nipped my bottom lip lightly with his teeth and soothed it by sucking it into his mouth.

I hadn't realized we had reached his room until he set me on my feet just in front of a king-sized bed. We were watching each other, both of us breathing heavily. He unbuttoned the last few buttons of his shirt and shrugged it off. I kicked my heels off. I reached out and touched the center of his chest. He was all muscle, not an ounce of fat on him. He was hard and lean with his real eight-pack abs that looked as if they had been sculpted. My very own Latin hottie!

He grabbed my hand and brought it to his lips, kissing my hand. Keeping my hand in his own, he prompted me to turn my back to him. The house had a fair amount of windows and his bedroom was no different. I felt him pull my hair to the side and I bent my head forward slightly. I looked over the bed while I felt his hands move to the zipper of the dress as he held one side and moved the zipper with the other hand. There was a mirror in the headboard and I could see my hips in the reflection. The only thing I was wearing underneath was a black thong.

He slid the dress off me and threw it to an ever increasing pile on the floor. He said softly, "Damn."

I glanced over my shoulder at him. He was dressed in his slacks only with a very noticeable tent in the front.

"Spread your legs and lean forward."

I was trembling and a little hesitant as I spread my legs and leaned forward with my hands on the bed.

"That's it, baby. Do you know how often I have imagined what you would feel like in my arms? What you would taste like?"

I had forgotten my nervousness until now. Through the mirror I could see how vulnerable I was in this position. I could see him behind me staring at my rear end. It had been so long since I had been with anyone sexually.

He reached out and caressed one ass cheek, squeezing softly. "Just like this baby," he said as he nudged me to one bended knee on the bed.

I licked my lips nervously. "Seva ... "

"Ssshhh. Trust me, baby." His eyes met my own in the mirror. "I won't hurt you. I promise. But you have to trust me." He stroked my hip and rubbed my backside.

Trust me, he says. Trust the same man that never called, that never spoke to me 'til now. I had trusted Adrian blindly before. I was going into this with my eyes wide open, wasn't I?

Seva's words echoed in my head, "Give us tonight." I took a deep breath. I wanted this. I so wanted this. There was nothing wrong with admitting who and what I wanted. That included acting on it as well. I closed my eyes for a moment. Seva waited with his hand on my hip.

I opened my eyes and gazed into his through the mirror. "Okay!" Not only was I answering him but I was telling myself, too. It would be naïve of me to think that he wanted something more than just tonight. So if tonight was all we had, then I would enjoy it as much as possible.

"Wider."

I spread my legs wider and waited to hear his pants hit the floor. I tried to will myself to relax. His hands left me and I started to turn to look for him when I felt the bed move. Seva slide down low so that his head was resting on the bed. I heard him breathe in deep as he used his hands to tilt my hips to his mouth. He made some sounds like, "Mmph." I felt him use the tip of his tongue to lick my center.

I sighed with delight.

He sucked hard and drove me wild with sensation. He swirled his tongue around and around with light brush strokes while I rotated my hips to get closer. I shivered with anticipation and worked my hips against him trying to get just the right angle. He thrust his tongue in and out like a piston and moaned. I squirmed and panted. The man knew how to work it.

I bent forward and looked down my body at him as he matched my rhythm. I gasped. He was gazing back at me and in those eyes I saw the flame that lit my fire.

I closed my eyes and trembled from head to toe. Breathless, my tongue trailing my top lip, I managed to get out, "There. Right there."

He moaned and squeezed my ass. The vibration of the moan resonated through my entire body, putting me right on the edge, right on the brink. He brushed my folds with his fingers, and then inserted one. My breath hitched.

He added a second finger and used his tongue in syncopation, creating the perfect rhythm. I shook my head, trembling now. Too much sensation. Too much. "Seva ... Se—"

The last syllable was lost in a scream as I climaxed, no doubt drenching his fingers in my cream. He stilled his tongue and sucked my inner thigh and slid from under me.

I felt like I was floating.

"Baby, you are so sexy. So hot."

All I could manage to respond was to say, "Mmm." I glanced behind me at him. He was naked ... and beautiful. Chocolate caramel muscle toned body, his manhood jutting up long, strong and proud from his body. His hips were tilted forward and he was making long strokes as he pleasured himself. I watched him, my eyes half lidded, as he slid in and out of his fist.

"You make me so hot," he whispered.

Ditto. I licked my lips and wriggled my finger at him. "Come here."

"I'm ready for baby. I want you so bad."

"Not before I taste you."

"M'kay ... Don't you move, though."

"Not a muscle," I said with a grin. He walked over to me and gripped his penis right at the base. I watched as a pearl drop formed right on the tip. I reached out to touch it.

"No hands, baby," he said breath heavily, stroking up his shaft. He reached out and caressed my bottom lip. "Just your mouth."

He painted my lower lip with the tip of his precome at the tip of his penis. "Open, baby."

I looked up at him as he angled his hips to slip past the "O" formation I had made with my lips. Goddamn he was gorgeous. Mentally I reminded myself to send a prayer up to the Latin gods later. He was smaller at the tip and then progressively wider. I tried to fit as much as I could but could only fit a couple of inches. I sucked, rocked and swirled my tongue back and forth. I watched his nostrils flare as he sucked in a deep breath. You heard an audible pop as he stepped away from me.

"You ready for me, baby?" I nodded. "Oh yeah."

"I want you to watch me, baby. Watch me in the mirror. Can you do that?"

"Mmm hmm."

He stepped up behind me and placed his hands on my hips. I closed my eyes. I was completely ready to be focused on sensation when he slapped me on the ass. "Hey!"

"Watch!" he commanded. He applied a little pressure on my back and I arched my back and jutted my ass up higher. He rubbed between my folds back and forth with just the tip his member, spreading my cream on him. A shiver spread through my body. Involuntarily I flinched and tensed up.

"Relax baby. Just feel." I felt him flex his hips as he held mine. I took a deep breath.

He entered me. I gasped. He was wide but so good. It was like Grand Canyon wide but decadent rich chocolate with triple fudge icing good. I watched him in the mirror. His head was bent, his mouth fashioned into a silent "Ooo."

God, that was hot. I felt myself cream even more. I caught my own reflection and barely recognized myself. My lips were kiss swollen. My cheeks were flushed. My dark hair rippled down in soft waves. I watched as my breasts bounced with every powerful stroke.

He set the rhythm, slow and steady. I wanted more. I flexed my hips to urge him on.

"Slow down, baby. We got all night."

I reached back and grabbed his wrist and held it, squeezed it until he watched me back in the mirror. "Wwaannt more. Hhharder."

"Baby, I—"

I didn't give him time to finish before I started moving my hips faster. I was close, tightening around him already. I knew he was holding back. His jaw was clenched and his eyes glittered. We were watching each other and I could feel him get harder and knew he was close to orgasm. I wanted to give him as much as he had given me. I clenched around him as hard I could and watched him throw back his head in abandon and give in. He lost control and fucked me, swinging his hips back and forth. He reached up and held me by the shoulders and pumped his hips against me. I heard him whisper over and over, "Mio ... mio."

"Ah, ah, ah." I fisted the sheets and felt him hit all my spots, even those I didn't know I had. *It had never been like this!* He lifted my hips high, my knees nearly lifted off the bed. Still I kept pace with him. That's when my orgasm hit. I convulsed and shook, clenching and unclenching around him. My orgasm triggered his own.

He came so hard, gripping my hips hard to the point of bruising. "Ah ... Baby!" he yelled.

I smiled, floating on the waves of pure pleasure.

Finally he released me and I dropped onto the matrress, breathing heavy. He lay down beside me and caressed my back. After awhile he spoke, "Are you okay, baby?"

I didn't answer at first. I was still trying to catch my breath.

"Mara?" Seva sounded concerned.

I turned to give him a lazy smile, like the one the cat has after drinking all the cream. "So good." It was all I could manage to get out. I wanted to let him know that it had been amazing. Mind blowing, even.

"We have all night, baby. I lost control at the end. I wanted to take my time with you but you—I knew you would make me crazy." He dropped a kiss on my shoulder.

My limbs felt like they weighed a ton, but I had to make sure he knew how I felt. I caressed his face and kissed him tenderly, putting into the kiss everything I had been trying to avoid from admitting.

I loved him. Plain and simple. I don't know when I fell for him exactly and it didn't matter. I was a goner and I wanted more than just one night.

"I loved it. Absolutely loved it. My body feels like jelly right now." I paused to smile at him. "Don't hold back, ever. I want it all, Seva. All of you. Not half. Just ... give me a few minutes," I said sleepily.

He chuckled and turned on his back and pulled me to him. I cuddled up against him, my thigh wrapped around one leg while I caressed his chest with my fingertips.

"I like how you touch me," he said softly.

"I like how you feel."

We were quiet for a while. I thought I might have been dreaming when he kissed my forehead and said, "Mine Mara. Mine. Never want to let you go. Nunca!"

I smiled.

My last thought before sleep captured me was *"What a nice dream."*

CHAPTER 14

I awoke alone bathed in the morning sunlight. I squinted and looked around the room. The walls were creme with tan curtains that fluttered in the island breeze. It was late morning and already warm. I hadn't noticed last night how the room was designed with a minimalist eye. Clean lines, simple glass table tops with no drawers, and shelving with rattan baskets was used to disguise clutter. The huge bed, large enough to easily accommodate three people, was the only splash of color in the room, covered in a striped orange patterned bedspread.

Seva, though deceptively lean, was a big man for his size. He was tall and my guess was that he was probably about 6'3, 6'4.

I sighed. *Speaking of big ...* I stretched. I was sore in places but it was a good sore. I grinned. My mind played back images of the night before as if it had been programmed for instant replay. True to his word, once hadn't been enough. We'd both woken up after the first time and I had been more than accommodating, eager even.

I thought back to the epiphany I had last night right before I drifted off to sleep the first time. I loved him. What happened to going slow? I crossed my arms and propped my chin on my hands and stared at myself in the mirror of the headboard. Despite my hair being disheveled, I didn't look too bad. Tousled and happy. There was a sparkle in my eye that I had to admit hadn't been there in quite a while. I giggled. I was smitten. I'm not sure when it happened either, somewhere between our first online chat and the last. I didn't think it was possible to fall for someone sight unseen but I had to admit I had been over the moon about Seva for the longest time.

My smile slipped. I leaned back on the pillows. What if he didn't feel the same? I thought back to his plea, "Give us tonight." He'd had his one night. He wasn't even in bed beside me. I could feel it coming but I hated to give into it. I wouldn't begrudge myself what had happened last night. It had been phenomenal but I had gone into this with my eyes wide open.

Right? A single tear trailed down my cheek.

I was not doing this. I was not going to cry over a man. Not another one. Even if he was drop dead gorgeous, and sexy, and perfect.

I quickly wiped another lone tear from my eye. I turned away from the mirror as if I could turn away from having to face myself. I whispered a silent prayer and slid out of bed. I could do this. There was no need for me to act like a sap.

"Dammit." I wiped both eyes free of tears and looked around the room for my clothes. I could only find Seva's shirt from last night. I hesitated for just a second and then slipped it on.

I made my way out of the sparse bedroom and headed for the stairs. It was a wide balustrade staircase that arced down into the living room. I must have been a little distracted not to notice. I loved details like that. Attention to detail was key in my business and sometimes the simplest things bought the most value to a home and sometimes the most expensive thing detracted from the home.

Apparently, my guy had style. I caressed the banister as I took the stairs. *My guy.* I swallowed quickly over the lump in my throat. Just go with the flow, I coached myself silently. Enjoy the time you're together. *Memories last a long time.*

I entered the kitchen and was greeted by the pungent smell of freshly brewed coffee and egg and sizzling bacon. My stomach rumbled with anticipation.

The kitchen had white walls in metallic décor with stainless steel countertops, tables and an island. At the center of the kitchen was the most incredible site of all.

Seva had taken a shower, his hair still in damp cornrows. He'd greeted me with a killer mega watt smile, dressed in a pair boxer briefs.

I slid onto the stool closest to him but away from the heat of the stove and crossed my legs. He flipped an egg in the pan and looked at me. "Hungry?"

"Mmm hmmm," I said and looked him up and down. I pursed my lips together with a barely contained grin and leaned on the counter to see more than just the top of his briefs.

"Me too," he said eyeing my bare legs. I blushed and poured myself a cup of coffee from the carafe on the counter. I scooped in five maybe six sugars and he raised an eyebrow at me. I pretended not to notice.

"Did you sleep well?"

I quirked an eyebrow up at him and drank from my mug. I set the cup down and licked my lips, his eyes following my every action. "Yes I did. What sleep I was allowed to get, I might add."

He chuckled in return as he made up the plates.

"Where are my clothes?" I asked innocently.

"Hanging in the closet where clothes are supposed to be," he answered with a smirk.

"Oh." My heart thudded. My clothes in his closet.

"Eat!" He placed my plate in front of me and leaned across the table to kiss me before he started in on his own dish. I kissed him back, though I couldn't help my knee jerk reaction.

I looked at him defiantly. "Ahhh. How about please?"

He smiled. "Please."

I relaxed and dug in. He'd made sunny side up eggs, bacon, and sausage with a bowl of cut fruit on the side. My heart softened. "Wow! This is amazing. Do you cook often?"

"Naw ... My roommate–," he began and hesitated. "Does most of the cooking," he finished quietly.

My heart squeezed. This was it. "Your roommate? A woman?" I tried to ask nonchalantly. I didn't trust myself to look at him so I took sudden interest in cutting the sausage with the side of my fork.

"No. A man."

"Oh." I smiled to myself. I hadn't realized that I had been holding my shoulders tight, preparing myself for the worst news. I relaxed. That was fine. "So, you're good friends?"

He nodded and looked down at his plate, "Yeah, you could say that."

We ate in silence for a few moments. I was watching him. He seemed tense for some reason.

"We should talk, you know," I said.

"I know. We should ... but later okay? I promise. Just ... later."

I looked at him. "Seva, promise me that you're not married."

He reached his hand across the table and intertwined our hands together. "I'm not married."

"And you're not engaged to be married?"

He grinned. "And, I'm not engaged to be married."

"Okay," I said with a curt nod. "We'll talk later."

Seva nodded but didn't move.

I disengaged my hand, finished eating and took my plate to the trash to empty remnants of my breakfast. I placed my plate in the sink, feeling at home in his modern kitchen, and turned to face Seva, trying to sound casual. "So, did DeVante accept the offer?"

I'd felt his eyes on me as I moved around the kitchen in his shirt that barely covered my bottom.

"Yep."

I glanced at him over my shoulder and turned back to the sink with a grin. His eyes felt hot on my body. "Were there any issues?"

"Nope."

"Why do I get the sense that you don't like him much?"

He got up to wipe down the stove and countertop. "That would be because I don't. That guy is an asshole."

My sentiments exactly. But I still had to do business with the man. Maybe Puerto Rico wouldn't be so bad, now that Seva and I had hooked up. I could handle DeVante, I decided.

Seva was still gazing at me, watching the hem of the shirt rise and fall with my movements.

Let's see if I can pique his interest, I thought.

"Where's the dish detergent?" I asked in my best coquettish voice.

"Und—" he cleared his throat and tried again. "Under the cabinet."

I smiled, squatted down, balancing on the balls of my feet, and reached under the cabinet. I was starting to have fun with this game just as I heard an unfamiliar male voice call out.

"Lucy, I'm home."

CHAPTER 15

I was numb. I was sitting on the bed in the same position I had been in for the last twenty minutes. I knew I was a bit in shock. Maybe I had been daydreaming. I pinched my leg. "Ouch." Nope. Not daydreaming. I was awake and it had been real ... more like surreal. I kept playing it over and over in my mind.

I had stood and turned toward the sound of the voice that rang out. Seva was standing stiff and definitely unhappy. I was puzzled. I looked to Seva for explanation. In walked a tall, tanned, man with shoulder length brown hair. I could only see his chiseled profile but I could tell the man was a looker, strong jaw, high cheekbones, an air of confidence about him. The stranger strode straight into the room and planted a kiss smack on Seva's lips. And Seva had kissed him back. He looked perturbed and he glanced at me uneasily. I was standing there with my mouth wide open staring from one to the other.

"Seva, who's the beauty? And why is she wearing your shirt?" the stranger said. "From the looks of it, that's about all she's wearing."

I looked down. No, this cannot be what I think it is. I closed my eyes and thought back to the kiss. Brief though it was, it had been fond. A kiss familiar. I was mortified. My cheeks were flaming.

"Mara—" Seva began.

"Excuse me," I said and practically ran for the stairs. I heard hushed angry whispers from the kitchen but I never stopped. I ran up to Seva's room and slammed the door shut. I paced first, cried, tried to stop crying, and cried harder.

Now, I was just ... I didn't know what to think. I wasn't sure how I was supposed to feel. My brain was in overdrive. He was gay. He wasn't gay. He hasn't seemed gay all this time. All the online play we'd had. He hadn't come up here after me. Maybe he didn't care. I thought back to the way he touched me. It had been sensuous, sexy. It wasn't just sex. It had felt like we had something between us. Dammit.

You could never tell with one of those down low brothers. Oh my God, I was an idiot. I couldn't believe I fell for a down low brother. We had used a condom last night. He'd stop to put one on—a Magnum. Who knew they came that big?

Even as I ranted, it didn't feel right. Seva was not gay. He had to be bi-sexual. Bi. Two men together. In the same bed. Thoughts of them in bed seemed ... hot.

Oh God.

Picturing them in bed, waiting for me to join them seemed hotter. It had been my ultimate fantasy for the longest time, I finally admitted to myself. And here it was. Or could be. It was my staple fantasy ... the one I always went back to. I thought back to Seva's behavior at breakfast. He certainly acted like he desired me. What's more was the look in his eye when that guy came in. It was as if he was willing me to understand. I was pretty sure that guy was the FWB (friend with benefits). I had made the assumption that he must have been involved with a woman.

You know what they say about making assumptions.

I took a deep breath. Even though I was pretty sure what the situation was, I decided I'd give him the chance to explain.

I showered in the bathroom just off Seva's room, found my clothes in the walk-in closet and dressed. When I reached the middle of the staircase I saw that the stranger was waiting for me at the bottom of the staircase. I slowed my descent and approached the bottom steps cautiously. He was staring at me and I was glancing around the room. I was right. He was handsome. Clean shaven, green eyes, shoulder length brown hair, tan complexion, strong chin, and manly from the look of his broad shoulders and tall stature. His cologne was intoxicating, musky and rich. Instantly I wanted to get closer but I stayed on the landing.

"Where is Sevastien?"

He held out his hand to me. "He's giving us a little time to get acquainted. My name is Naldo, Renaldo Guzman."

I shook it. "Uh ... nice to meet you," I said. "My name is—"

"Amara. Amara Simmons. Real estate entrepreneur."

I nodded. "You have me at an unfair advantage. I don't know anything about you," I said stiffly.

"That's true," he said still stroking my hand. "Did Seva take you on a tour of the house?"

I was a bit taken aback at the change of topic but decided to play along. I shook my head back and forth to indicate no. His warmth seeped into me, taking a little of my edge off.

"Allow me then." Naldo motioned for me to follow him to the front veranda. I stepped out onto the porch and realized that the front of the house was just fifty feet from the beachfront. The whole house was above the beach. I could imagine for just a moment me in a bikini and Seva in trunks ... or lack thereof. I shook the vision off. Now that the deal was done there was no reason for me to stay the whole week. In light of recent events, it probably wasn't wise for me to stick around.

Naldo let go of my hand, slipped on sunglasses and stepped off the porch onto the sand. I paused and cocked my head to the side, watching him. He took long strides into the white sand then turned and faced the house and crossed his arms, peering up at the house. Curious, I walked out to join him and squinted as I turned around to take in the view.

I was astounded. The house was architecturally and visually stunning. No kidding. "Wow!" was all I could say.

He gazed at me with a small grin and raised an eyebrow. "It's good, huh?"

"Good? I don't think that's the word I'd use," I said. "More like stunning."

Across the front of the house, I walked to one side to the other and back to stand in the center so I could take it all in. It was a beauty. All cool modern elegance, curves and sleek lines. A two-story modern house shaped in a U, it was painted pale yellow to blend in with the beach, and trimmed in light blue to match the sky. White column supports connected the ground level walkway to the second story open walkway. An exterior stairway contained by elegant white ironwork that matched the staircase I'd been admiring inside the house curved to connect the two levels. The roof also curved in a wave like the ironwork and was also was trimmed in a light blue.

"I've never seen architecture like this," I said.

"I take it you like my work?"

I turned and faced him. "No ... " I said in disbelief. I turned back to the house and looked back at him. "You're telling me you designed this house?"

"Mm hmm."

"You're an architect?" All the little design elements that I had credited Seva with, the praise really belonged to him? "That staircase ... you? Wow. Really! The house is beautiful."

"Thank you! I don't know which I enjoyed more, your attention to the aesthetics or your reaction to me being the brains behind the vision."

I blushed, looked down, and then back up at him. He was tall. Not as tall as Seva but still ... tall. "Did you design the interior as well or did Seva?"

"Seva?" he asked with a raised voice. "Sevastien is an intelligent man but he could care less about a vaulted ceiling versus a plain one. Seva has a head for business."

My color deepened as I added mentally, "and a magnificent body for sin." I had my Hail Mary's on stand by. I glanced back at him and knew he could probably guess exactly what I was thinking. And probably knew that body very well. I shook my head slightly. I had every right to feel indignant, pissed off, betrayed but ... I wasn't. I'd felt upset earlier. But now ... I was curious. Hell, it was beyond curiosity. It was arousing.

His eyes were sparkling and his grin deepened, as if he knew what I was thinking about. He turned to the curving exterior staircase, called over his shoulder and motioned for me to follow him. "The tour continues. This way."

I watched his posture, his hands, his mannerisms. Very masculine. All strong definite gestures. This was no feminine male.

He was wearing an olive green button-down shirt and white pants, all in summer cotton. From the looks of it, he was bulkier through the shoulders and chest where Seva wasn't. He definitely lifted weights. His hands and fingers were long, nails manicured. Not over the top just conscious. Good hygiene. There was one thing for certain. The man had a nice ass. It was a bit high but just enough curvature to fit my hand perfectly. When he reached the top of the stairs he turned and waited for me. I was still wearing the dress from last night and the wrap had fallen off one shoulder. I barely noticed it had slipped until I looked up at him.

Renaldo's look was full of heat as he looked me up and down. He spoke, his voice husky, "Inanimate objects Seva could care less about really. But, he does have an eye for beautiful people, namely women."

Men too, I thought returning his gaze.

I wet my lips with my tongue. His lips parted on an intake of breath as his eyes followed the motion. He turned abruptly and walked down the patio. I caught up to him and walked beside him, not touching, but feeling his body heat as we continued on the wrap-around balcony. We stopped to lean against the railing. The morning light shimmered off the gentle surf. The warm wind blew in off the water twisting my hair wild around my face.

I could see myself out here lounging, sun bathing. A little color would look good on me. Not that either one of them needed it, though, one having a deep tan complexion, the other a warm brown.

"So, how long have you known Sevastien?" I watched Renaldo's profile.

He didn't look at me, just spoke in an amused voice, as if he had been expecting my questions. "Sevastien and I met when we worked together on a project in Atlanta. It was a strictly professional relationship. We got along well but he was dating someone during the project. About a year ago, we crossed paths again on a project in Puerto Rico. I jumped at the chance to go. Not because of him. You see I was born in the states. New York, but my mother is from here. She and I moved to Manhattan when my father passed. I had never been to my homeland but there was a real sense of coming home."

I nodded even though he wasn't looking at me.

Gulls screeched overhead on their way to find scraps at the restaurant. Young kids walked by one hundred feet down by the rippling water, laughing and chattering in Spanish.

Renaldo smiled but still didn't look at me. "The project was doing poorly until he came on board. He suggested cuts to be made, streamlined operation, and put restrictions on spending. I don't know if you know this or not but Seva makes quite the impression, you know. He's hard to forget," he said as he turned to look at me.

I gave him a lopsided grin. "That is an understatement, my friend."

"Yeah. I imagine that it is." He laughed. "Come on!"

We rounded the corner of the house and were at the back of the exterior balcony. I was speechless. The view was amazing. A green lawn unmarred by anything spread out all the way to a forest of dense green trees. Clear blue skies topped it all.

"Ama-zing!"

"Yeah. I agree," he smiled.

I leaned on the balcony. I was apprehensive about how to ask but I forged ahead anyway. "So, how ... long have you been lovers?"

He dropped his head, took a deep breath and walked over to me, squaring his shoulders. When he reached me, he placed one hand on the rail and took off his sunglasses to look me in the eyes.

"I was wondering how long it was going to be before you brought that up?"

I looked at him steadily and said nothing, just waited.

"I've had relationships with women and men and honestly, it's always left me wanting more. The male relationship leaves me missing the touch of a woman. With the female, I miss the dominance of a man. I like them both. Need them both. I don't know if you can understand. Shortly after the project started here, and I was here on a regular basis, Seva and I had an amazing night. And we hung out with each other on a regular basis, not always ending up between the sheets."

I wished I could borrow his glasses. Instead I turned to face the amazingly green lawn and braced myself against the rail with both hands. He could only see my side profile and half of that was hidden by my hair.

Naldo continued undaunted. "Seva doesn't put himself into a box. He just is. He's not gay. He's not straight. He is attracted to who he's attracted to. By social standards, most consider him bisexual, as well as myself. I'm in love with Seva. I don't know if he knows it. I've never said it. I thought there was a time that he was ready to hear it from me but it was right about the time that he started emailing a woman. Turns out that woman was you."

I turned my head quickly in his direction. I'm sure shock was written all over my face.

"He thought you were great. He talked nonstop about this amazing woman he had met online. That you were beautiful and funny. Professional but stubborn. Sexy and innocent. A beautiful package all rolled into one."

I bit my lip and looked back at the view of the forest. I hadn't realized it until now that I was holding my breath. It was nice to hear from someone that had known Seva and seen him from day to day. My intuition hadn't been off. He felt the same things I had felt. It was a relief but it was still a puzzle. I was sure I knew the reason why. I just wanted, needed to hear it. I waited and sure enough Renaldo continued.

"He made you sound too perfect ... like I could easily be replaced. I was jealous. I wanted to know as much about you as possible. I would log on after he had gone to bed and I read your emails and chats. Other than your profile picture on the site, I avoided any of emails that I thought contained pictures. I thought you might think it was creepy if we ever met in person."

"You think, huh?" I said. I wasn't sure how I felt about his snooping, stalking actually. I closed my eyes and listened as he continued.

"I didn't know which one of us wanted you more. I even went so far as to register to the site and sent you an email but you never responded. I wanted to know you for myself."

My heart sped up at that. Maybe my fantasy wasn't so far fetched ...

He sounded close. And there he was as I turned my head back to him. I felt his warm breath on my face.

"Do you know what your name means? Have you ever looked it up?" Naldo whispered.

"No."

"It means everlasting beauty. It's certainly appropriate for you."

He leaned in closer. "Have you ever thought about it? Ever considered what it would be like ... two men touching you at the same time?"

My breathing quickened. I didn't know if that was the surf or my pulse I heard pounding away.

He watched me, fully aware of my reaction. He held my neck and pulled me closer. I let him. He whispered just above my own lips, so close I could feel his breath on my face, "Two lips ... two mouths ... two tongues. Would you like that, Amara?"

He used his thumb to caress my lower lip, playing with the center of my lower lip, teasing me with almost inserting his thumb in my mouth. "Can you imagine the sensation?"

I trailed my hands up his arms. I looked from his lips to his eyes. I held his gaze as I used my hand to insert his thumb into my mouth. Then I closed my lips around it. I watched the heat in his eyes go from hot to blazing. His body was pressed up against my own and I could feel him hard against my thigh.

I gave him back his thumb.

"Does that answer your question?" I asked with a husky voice.

Our lips met together cautiously. He watched me as I watched him as we kissed. He sucked my bottom lip and licked his way into my mouth. He tasted sweet, like almonds. I moaned. I couldn't help my response.

He broke the kiss with a shuddered breath and bowed his head to my neck. I was trying to slow my breathing. I never expected to respond to him like that. I attempted to take a step back and his hands tightened on my neck. "We can both have him. Together. Say yes, Amara. Sweetheart, please."

I pulled back and looked at him. "Si!"

CHAPTER 16

Renaldo took me back in the house. The sun was setting. The warm wind caressed my skin. Island life was awesome.

Even though Renaldo was leading me I would have gladly followed my nose. The smell of dinner wafted toward me from the kitchen. Was this for real? Were they for real? Did the both of them want me? Really? I didn't want to think about what I was doing. I was eager to do just as Renaldo had suggested and feel.

We entered the kitchen. Seva was at the stove cooking. The smell of grilled steaks and vegetables filled the room.

"That smells great!" I said.

Seva looked up and noticed that Renaldo and I had our hands intertwined. Seva looked at Naldo and Naldo nodded his head. I wet my lips nervously.

"I didn't know how you take your meat ... " Seva began.

I couldn't help it. I pursed my lips together to try and hold back the grin but it didn't last.

"Seriously dude?" Naldo was working hard to keep a straight face.

I laughed out loud. The tension broke. I was thankful for the laughter. Seva flashed a brilliantly white smile. God, the man was hot. Naldo pulled out my chair and seated me.

"Usually I cook dinner." Renaldo looked at me. "Well, usually I do all the cooking. But I must admit, the man makes a mean omelet."

I finally found my voice and smiled at Renaldo. "Yeah. I got a taste of it this morning." I looked at Seva directly. "It was delicious."

"No big." Seva shook his head.

Naldo and I both snickered

"You two have problems," I giggled.

"He makes it so easy," Naldo said.

I smiled widely. "I know!" *This was easy.*

Seva ignored our jab and offered me a glass of wine. "Red right?"

I smiled into my wine glass. "That's right. Thank you."

We ate and throughout dinner the guys asked about my girlfriends. They seemed to be fascinated by all aspects of my life. Which admittedly, for once, was ... nice. Very nice. It felt so natural to be with these two. It was as though we had always been together in this comfortable way. Seva held my hand across the island during dinner and I played footsy with Renaldo at the same time. I was still highly aroused from the kiss with Renaldo and I tried to ignore the heat in between my legs.

I was just waiting for one of them to make the first move.

After we finished eating, Renaldo was leaning against the island while Seva took the dishes to the sink. I figured it was either now or never. My vote was for now. Right now.

I walked around the island trailing my finger along the table. Seva had his back turned to us as he did the dishes, so he didn't see my strut. I walked up to Renaldo. He started stroking my arm, elbow to shoulder and back, as if was trying to reassure me. He and Seva were talking about something but I had stopped listening a long time ago. I could hear only my own heart beart, my own breathing. I wanted them, the both of them in the worst way. And I was determined I was gonna have them—both.

Renaldo glanced at me. "Amara?"

I started unbuttoning his silk shirt. "Si senor?" I looked at him with a raised eyebrow and a seductive grin. I looked from one man to the next acknowledging that I had Seva's undivided attention. He wasn't washing dishes anymore.

"Watch," I said seductively. *How ironic that I chose the very word Seva had said to me the night before.* I paid attention to the important task at hand. Naldo played with my hair and caressed my bottom lip with a fingertip. I glanced at Seva. He was gripping the counter tops when I reached the button on Naldo's pants.

"Mara," Renaldo said, part sigh, part plea.

I whispered. "Shsh." I unzipped his pants and took in him hand. I stroked him back and forth, from root to tip. I felt him harden quickly as his hips involuntarily met my downward stroke.

"I'm not going to last if you keep doing that, honey."

I bit my lip, grabbed his shirt and yanked him to me. I leaned into Naldo and caught his bottom lip between my own. I nipped and stroked his lip with my tongue while I sucked loudly. I kissed him with an aggression I had never known before. I released his lips just in time to hear an audible groan. I don't know which one of them made the sexy sound. It could have been one or both. Didn't matter to me though. It was all so hot. Naldo was rock hard. His movements were no longer tentative. His feet were braced apart, and he was watching himself slide in and out of my fist. I turned to Seva and ran a fingertip over my swollen bosom.

"Mara ... be sure," Seva said in a warning tone.

"Oh, I'm sure," I said huskily. I slid down to my knees and looked up at Renaldo. His chest rose and fell rapidly. He reached down and stroked my cheek. He had his mouth open, and was breathing heavily. I caught his thumb and sucked on it, using my tongue to caress him. I continued to stroke him and his hips curled back and forth, matching my rhythm. I sat back on my knees to survey my handiwork.

From this angle I could really appreciate just how fit he was. A muscular chest and tan thick thighs, long member. He wasn't as big as Seva; my guess was about eight inches.

"Mara ... " Naldo said softly, using his fingers on the back of my neck to urge me forward.

I glanced at Seva and noticed his erection tented under his slacks. *Oh yeah, so sure.*

I leaned forward and took Renaldo in my mouth.

"Mmm." His taste was a surprising mix of almond and cream. His smell was intoxicating. I was lost in it.

He hissed as I worked him in my mouth a bit at a time. I looked up at Naldo and watched as Seva kissed Naldo on the lips. Seva kissed Naldo once more and licked his way into Naldo's mouth. I couldn't help the moan that escaped. Seva reached out and brought Naldo's hand to his own erection. Naldo twisted slightly and kissed him back with fervor as he unbuttoned Seva's pants. Seva's erection was molded to his body, so big and proud. As Naldo released it from the prison of Seva's underwear, it sprang forward and cleaved the air.

God, they were both a beautiful sight. Naldo took Seva in hand and Seva groaned into his mouth through a kiss. Naldo quickened his pace with his hips and I felt a fine tremor through his thighs. I knew he was close and I wanted him to come. I wanted to taste him, badly. I was slick from my own excitement. I doubled my efforts, pushing him closer and closer to orgasm. Seva yanked Naldo's head back and licked him from his throat to his ear and pinched his nipple. Naldo cried out but the sound was muffled by Seva's kiss. He slammed his hips forward and held onto Seva's shoulders as he was caught in the climax of sensation. His taste had been as sweet as I thought it would be.

"Ay Dios Mio!" Naldo exclaimed.

I looked to Seva for explanation. Seva re-tucked himself in his pants, reached out and helped me up from my kneeling position on the floor. Seva's lips brushed my earlobe as he whispered the translation to me, "Oh my God."

I raised my eyebrow. *My sentiments exactly!* Seva pulled me against him roughly and slid his hand around my bottom and squeezed. He smacked my butt cheek and grinned. "My turn."

I smiled. "Oh yeah."

Seva led me to a bedroom just off the kitchen. Naldo followed, a predatory look on his face. *Boys, boys ... there is enough of me to share.*

The guest bedroom was decorated plainly: tan walls, an abstract painting made up of colors in red, gold, and tan, a closet and a king size bed. I walked in and turned to face them.

They both stood at the door, watching me keenly, hungrily. I reached for my zipper at the back of my dress and held Seva's gaze as I slide down the zipper. I let my dress pool around my feet. I watched Naldo as I stood there in the room with a king size bed. My hair brushed my shoulders on one side. I wore nothing but my thong.

I felt Naldo and Seva caress my body with their eyes and imagined what they saw. Luminous skin, graceful neck, voluptuous breasts, flat tummy, flared hips, thick thighs, and smooth calves.

"Ella es Hermosa!" Naldo said, his voice full of wonder.

"Yes. She is ... very beautiful," Seva said without taking his eyes off me. "Mara, I want you completely naked."

Barefoot, Naldo slipped off his shirt. Seva had lost his shirt back in the kitchen and was toeing off his shoes. I slid off my thong and leaned across the bed, lounging on my side, waiting. I wanted this. I so wanted this.

They were a feast for my eyes, the two of them. They were Latin gods as far as I was concerned. I didn't know what I did to deserve them, even if it was for only one time. I looked to my right. Naldo was shucking off his pants. I looked to my left. Seva stroked himself through his pants. I was so excited. I didn't know if I was going to orgasm from just one of them touching me, much less two. My hand drifted over my body.

"Mara?" Seva said.

I looked at Seva. "Yes?"

He wagged his finger back and forth. "No touching. You'll miss the show."

I smiled and stretched my arms above my head. Seva's eyes widened with delight.

Naldo knelt before Seva and cast a smoldering look my way.

I leaned forward and bit my lip.

He peeled Seva's underwear down and took him in his mouth. I gasped slightly. Seva threw his head back and pumped his hips slowly. My mouth watered as I watched Naldo stroke him with a fist as he could only fit a few inches in his mouth. Seva held him gently at the neck and curled his hips into him carefully. Naldo moaned and went faster.

They were a sight behold. I squirmed.

I was watching them and Seva was watching me. Naldo set back and stroked Seva while he kept his eyes on me. They both looked at me and it seemed in that moment there was uncertainty in their eyes. I realized that the display was intentional. They wanted me to see them together. It was as though they were giving me plenty of opportunity to back out if I wanted. Fat chance of that happening. I was all in.

"I don't know that I've seen anything more gorgeous than the two of you together," I whispered.

Seva tapped Naldo gently. Naldo looked and Seva stepped away slowly, out of Naldo's grip and mouth. Naldo looked over to me and flashed a grin, like he knew something I didn't.

Seva swatted him. "Stop that!"

He moved over my body and kissed me. He kissed me like I had given him the greatest gift. I sighed and smiled into the kiss.

"The pleasure is all mine," I whispered.

"Not yet." Seva grinned and pushed me playfully down on the bed, spreading my legs wide. He eyed my sweet spot. "Pretty," he grunted before he dived between my legs, his lips hungry on my most tender area. I moaned.

Naldo leaned across the bed and captured my nipple in his mouth. I brought my hands up to his head and held him to my breast. "Aahhh." I was lost in sensation. One mouth was demanding and the next was teasing. Naldo licked one breast and squeezed the other. I was close, so close. Seva seemed to read me so well. At just the right moment he inserted a finger and moved it back and forth. I was pumping my hips to match him, shaking my head back and forth.

"I can't ... Seva ... can't. Please ... "

Seva inserted a second finger and started stroking me with both fingers. Naldo bit a little harder as Seva went faster. My orgasm hit and I bucked. Seva wrapped his arms around my hips and never stopped. Naldo fell back and watched as I fought for air and begged for him to stop.

"Seva! Too much. Please!"

He growled a protest and continued to lick my most sensitive area over and over. I gasped as a second orgasm hit and I was literally floating.

As I settled back into my body, I felt Seva cover my body with his own.

"This is far from over," Seva whispered. "Open wide for me baby."

I gladly complied.

Naldo was lying beside us, stroking himself lazily. He reached out and intertwined our hands. Seva rubbed himself in between my folds, coating himself in my juices. He gazed at me as he pushed his way inside. I gasped and squeezed Naldo's hand. Seva reached down and played with my most sensitive area with his fingertips. My gaze unfocused and I could feel my body starting to clench around him already.

"That's it baby. Just feel," Seva said.

He flexed his hips slowly and I met him stroke for stroke. I felt Naldo's hand in my hair urging me to turn to him. He sucked my bottom lip in his mouth. Naldo broke the kiss and rose up on his knees. His erection dangled, jutting straight out from his body.

Seva's rhythm changed and became harder, more insistent. Memories of the very first night I had fantasized about him in the bath played through my mind. This was so much better that what I had imagined. I reached out for Naldo, encouraging him to come closer. I watched Seva's face as I reached out and touched Naldo. Naldo bit his lip and stroked his nipple. Seva's breathing quickened and he used shallow strokes while watching the two of us.

I encouraged Naldo to lie on his side. I took him into my mouth and he undulated his hips back and forth in and out of my mouth.

"Oh yeah baby," Naldo said.

I moaned at the sweet almond taste of him. So sweet.

Seva was breathing heavily as he said, "Fuck yeah."

Seva started shafting me deep, gripping my hips and hitting my G-spot. Naldo held my head in place as he curled his body around me to get a better angle. I watched Seva, his body glistening with a fine sheen of sweat. He was watching Naldo and I back and forth. Seva palmed one breast and Naldo palmed the other. They both matched a rhythm that complimented the other. Our movements started to be become frenzied. Naldo came first and hard, gasping out my name. I released him from my lips and Seva bent over and captured my lips savoring the Naldo's taste in my mouth. He rode high on my body, making sure to rub against my clit.

"Come ... with ... me baby," he said breathless.

I whimpered. I was so close.

"I can feel it, baby. Feel you so tight around me. Almost ... there ... Mara, NOW! Come for me now!"

My cry this time was soundless as my body was racked with orgasm after orgasm. *How did he do that?* I fell into a place of mindlessness. My body tingled all over.

Seva lay down and pulled me against him, so we were hugging chest to chest. Naldo spooned me from the back, his arms wrapped around both me and Seva. I never felt more protected.

We lay there, the three of us, panting, hearts pounding, sweaty bodies, warm and sweet.

I think that was the best sex of my life. But my mouth couldn't form the words to tell them, so I just soaked up their heat and breathed in their musk.

The distant surf hummed in the distance. Time floated by.

"Mara," Seva said in my ear after some time.

"Hmm," I said and I wiggled my bottom against Naldo. Naldo chuckled in the other ear.

"I need to tell you something," Seva breathed.

"Sleep first, talk later. Or round two later. Talk much much later," I said sleepily.

Seva nipped my ear. "I like how you think, but seriously—"

"Mmm." Whatever he was doing with his tongue was sending familiar tremors in delicate places.

"I need to tell you why I never called," Seva said softly.

I opened my eyes to give him my full attention. He sighed and sat up in bed putting his back against the headboard, putting distance between us. Naldo sat up and laid across the bed. I sat up too, and pulled the sheet with me as I leaned back against Naldo. I sat with my knees pulled up against my chest, my hands clasped together over my knees, and started making circles with my thumbs. God, this was gonna kill me. Naldo rubbed the small of my back, as if to reassure me.

I put up a brave front that I didn't feel and said, "Hit me with it." My body still tingled from our time together. I shivered.

Seva puffed out a breath and looked at the white wall straight ahead. "I never considered myself fitting into a box. I'm just me whether that means I'm attracted to a man or a woman or both." He turned to me. "I found that I've been attracted to both." He waited, searching my face, looking for some indication that I didn't understand.

I nodded to show I was listening.

He continued. "In some respects my relationship with Naldo was a surprise to me and in some ways it wasn't."

He looked down at his hands and then back up at me. "For many years when I imagined the future, it was with a wife and children. Me and Naldo—it was unexpected and for a while, I chose not to examine it. I was content to just let things be. Naldo and I had relations and he was just that, a friend with benefits."

He looked at Naldo and said, "My feelings started to change and I didn't know what that meant. Am I gay? Am I not gay? Am I bi? I wasn't sure that I was ready to answer those questions for anyone, least of all for myself. One thing I didn't want to be for sure was a brother that touts himself to a straight up hetero and he's gets broke off by a dude every once and while. I was already registered to the site when I got this email from the prettiest woman I've come across in a long time."

I felt my cheeks burning, surely a deep pink blush, but looked at him steadily.

"You were not what I expected. All spunk and sass, business smart and funny. On top of all that you are sexy as hell. I wanted it all but I wasn't sure how to explain. Every time I envisioned the conversation, it never went well so I had myself convinced that I should leave you to a better man. One who could give you what you wanted." He looked pained when he said that last part.

I reached out and took his hand.

Naldo had been quiet until now. "God! What a bear he was to live with. You have no idea. I've heard women say that men have periods. He seemed to be on his for the last couple of months."

"There you go with that." Seva smiled.

The two shared a warm smile.

Seva reached out and stroked my arm. I grasped his hand and squeezed. He squeezed back and let go of my hand. He took a deep breath. He wasn't finished. I waited. He finally spoke.

"You never know if the person you meet online is really the person they say they are, if the picture they send you is really them, or if they're telling you the whole truth. When you stepped into that conference room and I could see that you were everything you portrayed yourself to be ... I wanted you—badly." Seva propped up a knee.

"What I'm suggesting is certainly unconventional and there aren't many women that would take a chance on something like this."

I wasn't *many women*. Maybe he knew I would take a chance. My eyebrows furrowed. *Wait a minute, how did he know I would?*

"Let me finish," he said.

I realized the confusion showed on my face so I tried to have as blank a stare as I could have.

"I ... I didn't know if this would work. If you would accept me ... us ... like this. If it wasn't cool—" He took a deep breath and looked me in the eye. "I didn't think I could deal with you not wanting me."

I stilled my breathing.

"A year ago, I fell in love with a man. Three months ago, I fell in love with a woman and I want them both. I want you two be my lovers, my partners, my best friends, and my confidants. I want to come home to the arms of both of you knowing that I've found peace, love and happiness in two of the biggest pain in the asses ever—'cause you're just letting me go on here. Can a brother get a break?"

Naldo and I both laughed.

"Well, let me pick my jaw up off the floor why don'tcha. Did I just hear you right?" Naldo asked.

I looked at Naldo, "Did you hear ... ?"

"I do believe I did ... but did you hear that bit about ... ?"

"Yeah, I heard that too ... "

I looked back at Seva and I crawled over to his side. "Well sure, silly 'cause you know ... I love you too."

Seva beamed and gave me a brilliant smile. Naldo joined us, and snuggled on the other side of Seva. His eyes were shining as he looked at Seva and said, "You know I ... "

Seva reached up, grabbed him by the neck and pulled him down for a quick kiss. "I know ... "

Naldo settled back against the pillows with a content look on his face. Seva looked at me and pointed to Naldo on the other side of him.

"You'll get used to him. He'll have someone to talk to about a Mockler faucet opposed to a retro."

Naldo said in exasperation, "That's Kohler dude. Kohler!"

Seva waived his hand. "Whatever!"

He sobered and looked at me. "So you'll stay?"

"As if." I saw the smile start to slip from his face. I reached up and kissed him tenderly. "As if you could get rid of me."

"Sometimes dreams do come true, huh?"

"Yep, and fantasies too!"

EPILOGUE
Six months later ...

"Which one of these fine Latin hunks is your man, Mara?" Nessa asked out of the side of her mouth, shaking Naldo's hand first, then Seva's. I hadn't really filled her in on the situation, having been so busy with traveling back to California once a week and packing things up a bit at a time to take back to Puerto Rico which was now home. Nessa kept Seva's hand just a little bit too long for my taste but I was gonna let it go. Honest. Seriously. Okay maybe. Okay, she had one more time to touch my man and I was gonna let her have it.

It was Fourth of July weekend and I had invited the girls down to spend some time with me and my men.

"Both!" I said as I set the pitcher of lemonade on the patio table.

Nikki and Stacey looked up from the plate of hors-d'oeuvres, eyes wide with disbelief, and said in unison, "Both?"

Naldo nodded at the two with a little smile, "Dos!"

"We get the picture," Adrian said from the staircase.

I heard Nessa ask Katie between clenched teeth, "Who in the hell invited him?"

"Adrian!" Ignoring my friends I beamed, rushed over and gave Adrian a hug. I glanced behind him and saw Naomi. If looks could kill, I'd be a dead duck.

Adrian squeezed me back and breathed in my scent. He whispered, "You still smell good."

"Adrian," I said as a warning between clenched teeth. I excused myself from Adrian's arms and greeted Naomi.

"It's wonderful of you to come. Did you enjoy the plane ride?"

"It was fine," she answered tersely. *Right!*

"Would you like some refreshments?"

"I'm sure my hus-band will bring some over to me." She lowered her voice and added, "That is if you can keep your distance." I was not going to ruin a perfectly good get together by laying into her. I wasn't ... well, maybe. But not right now.

"So Mara, you permanently moved down here to the islands?" Stacie asked.

"Yep. I'll be renting out my house. You will take over the California office and I will run things from here."

"Why not let me take it and keep it in the family so to speak? That way when you come home, you can just come home," Katie said.

"Aaw." Nikki and Nessa teased. I looked at my guys lounging by the bar we had set up. They looked fabulous standing side by side. I asked their opinion silently with a raised eyebrow. Naldo shrugged. Seva nodded.

"Mara, what's the name of that spa that client of yours opened on the island of Culebra?" Charlie asked.

"Kpasa."

"Me speaka no Spanish. What does that mean?" Charlie asked.

Seva chimed in. "It means 'what's up?' "

"There are plans for a casino and all. We just finished the conservation and environmental study so it will be a while yet before the casino is finished but I'll let you know when it happens. I actually can get you guys in for a full day in the spa courtesy of Mr. Eric DeVante."

"Hey Seva! What do you think of DeVante?" Katie asked

"He's a prick," he answered back with a smile.

"I don't really think he's that bad," Michael said.

"Of course you would say that, Michael. I neva heard you say a cross word about anybody," Katie said.

Michael huffed and pushed his glasses back up on his face and muttered, "There's a first for everything."

"I heard that," Katie said. She took a swig of lemonade and started making faces at the taste.

I was already giggling.

"You guys let her near the sugar jar again, didn't cha? Don't you guys know you're dealing with a sugar junkie? I'm talking about a habit here, people." Katie gave it her best concerned expression.

"We try to appease the beast," Naldo said.

I shook my finger at them good-naturedly. "Beast eh ... Wait'll you get a load of my claws."

Naldo grinned. "Bring it on!"

"So what's next for you? Children?" Adrian asked.

I paused and glanced at the guys. I swear Seva's eyes started glittering at the thought. Naldo had a little secret smile. "Never say never." I shrugged.

"Wait! So let me understand this. You are dating both of them and now you're talking about having children. Where did you meet these men?" Naomi said.

"We met on a site called betterthan8.com. Charlie suggested the site," I said.

Naomi's eyebrows went up. Charlie blushed and said to her, "If you weren't married, I'd tell you to check it out. The site is pretty awesome."

"And eight stands for?" Naomi asked.

"I'm sure you can use your imagination." I smirked.

"And you guys work ... as a couple?" Naomi asked with disbelief.

I walked over to my guys and kissed Seva on the lips and then Naldo. "No dear." Okay, so I let dear drip with sarcasm. "We work as a threesome."

Nessa looked at us and cocked her head to the side, "You guys almost look like an Oreo."

"Nessa!" Stacey exclaimed.

"What? I'm just saying ... " We three looked each other over and grinned.

Seva whispered in my ear, "I think you look pretty good."

I turned my head to meet his kiss and said, "I think you do too."

Naldo moved my hair back and murmured, "Good enough to eat" before he sucked my neck just behind my ear.

Nessa interrupted and said, "Seva I thought you were looking for a sista. I happen to know one fine, available, sexy, show-a-brother-a-good-time kinda lady."

Seva turned and gave her a sly lazy smile with a raised eyebrow. "Didn't you know, Nessa? I already have one. Mara's mixed."

Nessa's smile slipped and she looked at me. "Huh." I shrugged apologetically

Naldo nuzzled my neck and Seva used his finger to turn my face up to him. He stared down into my face as he stroked it. "Her mother was black and her father was white. She's quite the chameleon." He leaned in and kissed me again.

"Really?! Mara! You never said."

"You never asked."

I turned and looked at her with a half smile. "Both my parents are gone now. It's just me but yeah, I am and no, I don't make it a point to tell people. I like for them to think what they will." I shrugged. "It usually works for me."

"And you've moved to Puerto Rico permanently?" Adrian asked, narrowing his eyes slightly.

"Well duh silly, how else are you gonna be with the people you love?" I said waving my hands around to include everyone on the patio.

Nikki perched her hands under her chin and said, "Swoon! That is soo romantic!"

"Lord, have mercy!" Katie said with an eye roll.

"Mara? Was it worth it?" Charlie asked.

"Abso-freakin-lutely!"

ABOUT THE AUTHOR

An avid reader all her life, Erin Jamison dreamed of telling stories of her very own. Mustering her bravado, she forged ahead to create stories that promote individuality, confidence, fearlessness, fortitude and passion. She writes sensual stories of women for women who want a bit of a thrill and who know what they want and aren't afraid to go after it. Watch for more *Better Than 8* stories! She loves to hear from her readers at erin@erinjamison.com. You can also visit her site for extras at http://www.erinjamison.com/.